THE FLAME

The aristocratic Mexican Román Castillo might be a very attractive man—he *was* a very attractive man, Laura had to confess!—but wouldn't she be a fool to think of marrying him? For no woman, it was clear, not even a wife, would hold Román's interest for very long . . .

Books you will enjoy
by ELIZABETH GRAHAM

VISION OF LOVE

Pressured by her editor to get a story on the elusive millionaire Mitch Gardner, who had recently become her aunt Adele's neighbour, Kelly went reluctantly to visit her—only to be pressured by the old lady 'to make a match of it' with him! And even if Kelly had felt like complying, wasn't Mitch already rather obviously involved with the far more suitable Vanessa Walsh?

HIGHLAND GATHERING

When her father's brother died, Fiona Mackay assumed that her father, as his nearest relative, would be the heir to his Scottish castle. But it was also likely that her uncle's stepson, Roderick Cairns, would consider he had certain rights, too. However, if Roderick imagined that the solution would be for him to marry the new heir's daughter he could think again! So Fiona went to Scotland, ready to do battle—only to find that the situation wasn't at all as she had imagined!

THE FLAME TREE

BY

ELIZABETH GRAHAM

MILLS & BOON LIMITED
15–16 BROOK'S MEWS
LONDON W1A 1DR

All the characters in this book have no existence outside the imagination of the Author, and have no relation whatsoever to anyone bearing the same name or names. They are not even distantly inspired by any individual known or unknown to the Author, and all the incidents are pure invention.

The text of this publication or any part thereof may not be reproduced or transmitted in any form or by any means, electronic or mechanical, including photocopying, recording, storage in an information retrieval system, or otherwise, without the written permission of the publisher.

This book is sold subject to the condition that it shall not, by way of trade or otherwise, be lent, resold, hired out or otherwise circulated without the prior consent of the publisher in any form of binding or cover other than that in which it is published and without a similar condition including this condition being imposed on the subsequent purchaser.

*First published in Great Britain 1985
by Mills & Boon Limited*

© Elizabeth Graham 1985

*Australian copyright 1985
Philippine copyright 1985
This edition 1985*

ISBN 0 263 74993 2

*Set in Monophoto Plantin 11 on 11½ pt.
01–0385 – 48370*

*Made and printed in Great Britain by
Richard Clay (The Chaucer Press) Ltd,
Bungay, Suffolk*

CHAPTER ONE

THE Villa Castillo seemed tailor-made for her purposes, Laura Benson thought as she leaned forward eagerly in her seat while the driver went to open the elaborately arched wrought iron gates. The mansion's pale grey façade had turned to dazzling white in the clear penetration of afternoon sun, which slanted shadowed areas under the raised roofs of turret-like belltowers flanking the impressive Mexican-Spanish edifice.

Laura would have preferred to walk up the short horseshoe-shaped driveway to the wide, shallow steps leading up to the massive studded entrance doors, but she knew that the chauffeur— at the airport he had introduced himself as 'the chauffeur from the Villa Castillo'—would frown on such independence, having been instructed to deliver her to her hostess's doorstep. She caught a glimpse of meticulously cared for grass and flower borders edging the cement-topped drive-way, and then she was sliding across the beige suede of the rear seat and stepping out on to the paved area before the steps.

'*Muchas gracias,*' she thanked the gravely courteous middle-aged driver who held the door for her. She had been pleased to find that the language she had used with fluency as a child hadn't deserted her completely. While Manuel went to retrieve her luggage, she started slowly on the upward climb to the somewhat overwhelming entrance doors, a smile already forming on her lips for the woman who would greet her there. Her hostess was Señora Isabel Castillo, a close friend of her mother for many years.

The right-hand door swung open noiselessly as she approached, but the woman who greeted her with a shy smile was dressed in the sombre black and crisp white apron that denoted her status as an employee.

'Please pass,' she said in awkward English, indicating with a hand the gloomy depths of an interior hall, her face breaking into a pleased smile when Laura thanked her in Spanish. Rapidly, she went on, 'I will show you to your room immediately. The Señora will meet you for *merienda* in the small *sala* at four.'

Laura nodded and walked further into the hall, while the maid spoke quickly to Manuel as he came in with her luggage. The small pang of disappointment she felt at not being met at once by her hostess was quickly dissipated as her eyes became accustomed to the dimmer light in the hall and took in its elegant splendour. Cool pale marble flooring gleamed richly on its way to two grand staircases that divided the huge entrance hall. They were of marble too, but vivid red carpeting swept up their centres to an upper floor. Laura's heels echoed as she walked slowly on, glancing up to see that the hall was unceilinged until it reached beyond the second storey. It was like being in a vast, echoing and hollow cathedral. The Castillo family obviously wasn't one to curl up cosily with a book, she thought wryly, although the other rooms were perhaps less awe-inspiring.

The sound of running water attracted her attention to the centre of the hall, and she gave a soft exclamation as she went forward to a pure white marble fountain with its four shy boy statues who spouted water into the smooth shallow bowl surrounding them. Someone in the family must have, or have had, a sense of humour. The faint smile stayed on her lips as the maid came up behind her, trailed by the wiry Manuel carrying her luggage.

'If you will follow me, *señorita*, I will take you to your apartment.' She went towards the left staircase and started up, seeming to have lost some of her shyness as she turned occasionally to the following Laura. 'My name is Rosa, and the *Señora* has told me to help you in any way I can. You have only to ring the bell in your room.'

About to thank her again, Laura halted abruptly at the top of the stairs when a door was flung violently open further down the hall and angry voices billowed towards them.

'I won't go into the office at all if you don't stop this nagging, Mamá!' a man shouted, his voice pitched high with anger. 'You're getting to be as bad as *he* is!'

'You would not speak to me like this if he were here,' an older woman's tones faded to inaudibility with her last words.

'He is not my father, he has no rights over me! I warn you, Mamá, one of these days I'll walk out of here and take a place of my own!'

Wearily, the older woman retorted, 'And what would you live on, my son? You can be sure——' Her voice was cut off again, this time by the slamming of a door.

Embarrassment flooded Laura as a well-dressed, handsome young man careened along the corridor towards them; knowing that his temper tantrum had been observed would surely increase his anger. But he went striding past the trio as if they didn't exist, and moments later his heels rang loudly as he crossed the marble hall below.

'Señor Nicolas,' Rosa explained with a calmness that suggested the scene they had just witnessed was an everyday occurrence.

Laura hastened to catch up with the maid's renewed pace, her mind whirling with thoughts of what was happening now mingled with almost forgotten memories. *Nicolas*—long ago, in Mexico City, her mother had taken her to visit the Señora who was now her hostess . . . and once or twice Laura had briefly met the Señora's son, who was a year or two younger than herself. *Nicolas*. From the sounds of it, he was still the spoiled brat he had been even then.

Rosa led her past door after door along the wide passageway, which was lit by stained glass windows contained in gothic arches on one side, the rooms lining the right placed furthest from the street noises she could hear dully through the stained glass. At the end of the corridor, Rosa threw open a door and stood back to let Laura precede her.

'Oh, this is lovely,' she exclaimed involuntarily in English, her gaze going delightedly from atmospheric black beams spanning the high white ceiling to the heavy Colonial furniture to the high lofted canopied bed with its rich hangings of red and gold tapestry cloth. Only occasional glimpses of marble floor were visible where the thick Aztec-gold carpeting didn't cover. 'Apartment' would have described it more accurately, she thought, than 'bedroom'. It was so spacious that the bedroom area didn't encroach at all on the rattan chairs and table arranged attractively before balcony doors like a separate sitting room. In a far corner adjacent to the sitting area was a leather-topped desk and padded office chair.

'Would you like me to unpack for you now, *señorita*,' Rosa reminded her of her presence, 'or will you rest first after your journey?'

Laura glanced at her watch; two-thirty. 'I have lots of time to do that before I see the *Señora*,' she smiled, 'and I may have a rest too. Where is the salon I'm to meet her in?'

'I will come for you at four.' Rosa hesitated as she passed the suitcases Manuel had helpfully hoisted to the long padded bench at the foot of the bed. 'You are sure?' she asked doubtfully.

'Really sure.' Laura longed impatiently to be alone to investigate her new surroundings, but her smile remained while she assured Rosa that she could manage.

The balcony doors did indeed lead to a balcony of sorts, though she discovered it was more like a terrace or patio with its red brick floor tiles and clay pots filled with tropical greenery; white wrought iron chairs and small table provided an outdoor seating area which overlooked a breath-takingly beautiful garden patio below, filled with flowers and fountains and joined by neatly paved paths joining each separate area. Most beautiful of all was the magnificent flame tree in full bloom that flanked one side of her balcony. The cup-like blossoms in fiery orange-red seemed to symbolise the challenge and beauty that was Mexico.

Gratitude rose up to overwhelm her as she took one of the balcony chairs and stared mistily down at the colourful gardens below, which were completely surrounded by the delicate grey interior walls of the mansion. Señora Castillo's generosity *was* overwhelming ... after all, she hadn't seen Laura since she was a child, and to respond so fulsomely to her old friend's request was positively noble.

Laura hadn't wanted her mother to impose on a woman she herself hadn't seen for some years; Laura had insisted adamantly that she could stay in a hotel or apartment close by and visit the Señora whenever convenient. But Eleanor Benson had breezily demolished her daughter's objections.

'Nonsense, Isabel won't mind a bit. She's often asked us to come and stay for a while, and she knows she's welcome to come to us at any time. Besides,' she reached for pen and notepaper, 'you'll get the proper background for your book if you stay with Isabel. Her husband's family goes back hundreds of years in Mexican history, and though I haven't seen the Guadalajara house, Isabel's told me enough about it that I'm sure it's just the kind of background you need for your book.'

Her book. Laura leaned forward and clasped her knees, a tentative smile touching her lips. It still didn't seem possible that she was the author of a successful novel, a first novel at that. Everything had happened so quickly after the initial interminable wait to hear the fate of the manuscript she had laboured over so long and hard. Even the usually sour critics had been kind, the most acerbic of all proclaiming the book 'a lightweight but eminently enjoyable first novel by a young woman who knows whereof she speaks. Her heroine's background is obviously based on her own as the daughter of a United States Consul and all that that entails. It remains to be seen if Miss Benson has what it takes to equally enchant us with her second novel.'

Laura had been well into plotting that second novel when she read that review, and it had had the effect of spurring her on to proving to the faceless critic that she could, indeed, do it again.

Although, she mused realistically now, it wasn't going to be easy. The first manuscript had flowed with satisfying ease—because, as the critic had pointed out, it had the solidity of her background behind it. There had been few difficulties in taking her heroine through what was virtually a re-run of her own nomadic existence as her father's daughter. Unlike her older brother, Mike, who had been sent back to the States for his education, Laura had travelled the world with her parents, sometimes attending special American schools and sometimes local educational systems. Hence her facility with languages—French, Italian, Spanish, even a goodly smattering of Dutch. Although she had attended the American School in Mexico City during her father's six years there as Vice-Consul, Spanish had become like a second language to her because of the friends she had there and the servants who spoke no English.

Her eyes fixed on the vivid papery blossoms of the flame tree, and she felt a pang of misgiving. *Could* she do it again? This book would be so

different from her first . . . after all, she had no
real experience in the problems her next heroine
would portray. How could she have? She had
never been married to a proud, arrogant Spanish-
Mexican who was ruthless in business, kind to his
many mistresses, behaved abominably to his wife.
Yet the man was so clear to her . . . she could see
in her mind's eye his olive-skinned features, his
cruel yet sensually attractive mouth, his arrogantly assured bearing. She had never known
such a man, but he was as real to her as her own
father.

Laura rose and returned to the comfortable
bedroom, dismissing her fictional character until
she could cope with him more freely. Now she
had to unpack and perhaps shower before
changing her clothes to meet with Señora
Castillo. The woman's voice she had heard
must have been hers, she conjectured as she
snapped open the locks of her first suitcase.
The young man, Nicolas, had called her
'Mamá', so it must be she. Would she still be
upset by her son's behaviour when she entertained Laura at tea an hour from now? Not that
Laura would blame her if she were—in her
understanding, Mexican men were normally
unfailingly polite to their parents. Nicholas
certainly hadn't been so to his mother.

The bathroom adjoining the bedroom drew a
rapturous sigh . . . tiny clay-coloured tiles
pattened the floors and the steps leading down
into the sunken tub of translucent marble. Lushly
growing tropical greenery outside the full-length
windows made the bathroom a private paradise,
and Laura lost no time in shedding the warm knit

fabric of her travel suit to test the waters of the Romanesque tub.

The small salon gave the impression of comfortable relaxation in its sofas and armchairs upholstered in bright chintz, its low tables of Mexican onyx, casually arranged bookcases and display shelves of bamboo, all reinforced by the smiling charm of the plump matron who rose to greet Laura.

'Ah, my dear,' she breathed dramatically, embracing Laura's much taller and more slender figure with emotional enthusiasm before holding her off to gaze mistily at her. 'You are even more beautiful than I expected! And so clever too! Who would have expected the little *niña* with her hair of fire and so thin legs to become a famous author!'

Laura's returned smile was slightly forced. Her mother's friends, the ones who had known her as a child, could never entirely dismiss the carroty gold of her youthful hair or the bony slenderness of her unformed body. Some of them, even though the hair had lightened to a sunlit gold, her body to an admittedly slender woman's but with all the requisite curves, found it impossible to separate the new from the old Laura. She hoped Señora Castillo wasn't one of those.

'Being famous as an author seemingly only lasts until the second book appears,' she denigrated, accepting the sofa corner her hostess indicated with a quick, graceful motion of her hand.

'Your second book—that is why you are here, yes?' Isabel Castillo questioned brightly, her dark eyes in plump olive cheeks scanning the blue of Laura's inquisitively.

'Mainly,' Laura admitted hesitantly, 'but I must admit to wanting to see if Mexico is really as wonderful as I remember it, or if just being a child here made it so.'

'Mexico *is* special,' Isabel nodded, seeming pleased. 'I have never been outside this country of mine, but many people have said this same thing to me.' She leaned forward and lifted the small gold bell from the low table between them, ringing it in a peremptory fashion that spoke eloquently of her aristocratic background. 'We will have tea, my dear, and you will tell me about your mother. It seems strange that we remain such good friends although it is many years since we met. What kind of tea do you prefer,' she digressed as a wide-eyed maid, not Rosa, came into the room, '*manzanilla* or *negro*?'

'*Negro*,' Laura chose haphazardly, listening while her hostess loftily ordered that and *manzanilla* for herself. No other directions were given, but when the maid reappeared moments later, she was wheeling a trolley replete with daintily cut sandwiches of thinly sliced ham, soft cheese, or golden brown pâté. The cup she accepted from Isabel's hand was exquisitely formed, and she felt vaguely ashamed of the raging appetite that made her take one after another of the ham sandwiches. It had been a long time since lunch on the plane.

Between bites, she answered the older woman's questions about her mother, telling her that Eleanor was at last growing tired of travelling constantly, making a home for a year or two in some alien environment before moving on to yet another. 'She would like nothing better than to settle in some place like Santa Barbara and live a normal life for a change.'

'But your father?' Isabel probed with raised black brows. 'Your mother must go with him wherever he goes, is that not so? In any case, I wonder if she would be satisfied with a normal life after so long the wife of a Consul, with everything that means. She would perhaps miss the excitement of social life, and the status she has as the wife of a prominent man.' The last was spoken wistfully, and Laura was reminded of her hostess's widowed status.

'Do you find your life lonely?' she asked impulsively, then went on less certainly, 'I mean, without your husband?'

'Enrique died seven years ago,' Isabel shrugged philosophically, 'and I have become adjusted to my widowed state. If he were still alive, I would be worrying about which dress to wear for which social function, but as it is,' she shrugged again, 'I have only my son, Nicolas, to worry about.'

Laura bit her lip, not knowing whether or not she should make known her unwitting eaves-dropping on the early afternoon scene. 'You only have one son?' she offered lamely.

The older woman's face softened luminously. 'Yes. We prayed for more children, but were blessed only with Nicolas.'

Blessed—or damned? Recalling the bitter young man's ugly treatment of his mother and the furious tap of his heels across the hall, Laura was inclined to favour the latter. Isabel, however, seemingly had no such doubts about her son's worthiness.

'Nico is taking his father's place in the family business,' she confided proudly. 'He is still young, of course, but I am confident even Román will be proud of him in the end.'

'Román?'

Isabel stared back at her with disbelieving snapping brown eyes. 'My nephew. Did your mother not tell you that I was left with nothing after my husband's death? Although Enrique gave his best years to the business, everything was passed on to his brother's son, Román. I say business, but there are many branches of it. I have lost count,' she said, adding wistfully, 'and I think Enrique did too. It was all too much for him.' She sighed, then a steely glint came into her eye. 'But Nico will succeed where his father failed. It is his birthright to share the family fortunes, and I will——' she paused and bit her lip before going on more neutrally, 'I have great hopes for him.'

'I'm sure you do,' replied Laura without a trace of the doubt that had filled her after overhearing Nicolas's petulant outburst earlier. To divert her hostess from an obviously painful subject, she asked idly, 'Does Román live in Guadalajara?'

Isabel frowned. 'Yes, of course.' She waved a hand towards the comfortably furnished room, her tone betraying bitterness as she said, 'Román owns everything you see here. The *casa*, the furnishings, even the chairs we sit on.'

Laura felt as if she had escaped on regaining her own room. From what? The question went round and round in her mind as she paced restlessly back and forth, wishing abstractedly that she had left her unpacking until now so that she would have something to do.

Darn her mother for not making the position clear! Why hadn't she spelled it out that she was to be the guest, not of Isabel Castillo, but the nephew who owned every stick and stone of the Villa Castillo? How could she possibly settle down to her writing knowing that she was the reluctant guest of a man who probably was unaware of her existence? And wouldn't care if he did know, by the sounds of him.

According to Isabel, he had gone to tend to business in Mexico City, where the principal offices were. He might return tomorrow, or he could conceivably stay away for weeks. All Laura knew at this moment was that she had no desire to meet him, to feel the lash of his righteous anger at finding an uninvited guest in his home. He was evidently unmarried, so there wasn't the added complication of a wife to contend with. The best course of action would be to glean her background material as speedily as possible and make her exit from the Villa Castillo.

But although she took her portable typewriter from its case and set it up on the leather-topped desk, she found it impossible to concentrate on characters or story line. She got up impatiently and went to the open doors to the balcony terrace, staring down into the courtyard gardens below. Her time until dinner at eight-thirty would have been better spent in investigating the old mansion, which dated back over two hundred years. Two hundred years of being handed down from one Castillo elder son to the next. And that thought brought her back to Román Castillo, the present owner.

Sighing, she turned back into the room, kicking off her sandals before lying down on the red and gold coverlet and blinking up at the bed's matching canopy overhead.

It was strange that a man like Román Castillo was not yet married, despite his age, which Isabel had told her was thirty-two. Most men with so much to hand down in the way of worldly goods made sure of the succession at a much earlier age. From what Isabel had let slip, there was no shortage of women in his life, eligible or otherwise. That information had come after the sad tale of how inconsolable he had been at the age of fourteen after his mother's death.

'His father,' the older woman had confided in a stage whisper, 'was not a soft man, like my Enrique. Juan felt Aña's death very much, but he was able to hide his grief, even from his son. They were so much alike, those two, that when Juan himself passed away, Roman, too, hid his feelings.'

Now, lying on the comfortably sprung bed, Laura felt a prickle of interest in her story. She could probably use Román Castillo's background as motivation for her implacably cold hero. . .

Only Isabel was present in the small salon when Laura found her way downstairs at eight-twenty. Her sleep, although it had been troubled by fitful visions of her hero's coldly chiselled features, had refreshed her.

'You look charming, my dear,' Isabel complimented, her purely female appraisal taking in the turquoise knee-length dress that fitted loosely and only suggested the slender lines of Laura's curves. 'Do you find it possible to believe that once I was almost as slim as you?' She looked wryly down at her own generous proportions in purple crêpe relieved by a sparkle of diamonds at throat and ears.

'I have the opposite problem,' smiled Laura, coming further into the room. 'Nothing I eat stays with me, and I guess when I'm older I'll be all skin and bones and wrinkles.'

'Oh no, no,' cried Isabel, 'once you have children you will have all the weight you want. Ah, here you are, Nico,' she looked beyond Laura to the door, 'just in time to pour us a drink before dinner. But first come and meet our guest, Laura Benson.'

Laura turned—and scarcely believed her eyes when she saw the immaculately dressed Nicolas come smiling towards her, his hand outstretched, effusive admiration in his mid-brown eyes. The petulant schoolboy of early afternoon had been transformed into a suavely cultured son any mother would be proud of. He took her hand and, instead of shaking it, raised it to his lips to kiss the backs of her fingers in an extravagant gesture.

'I am indeed pleased to meet you, Señorita Benson,' he murmured in English, his voice dulcet compared with its earlier bad-tempered tone. 'When my mother told me we were to expect a guest, I had no idea that she would be so beautiful, so charming, as you.'

Laura's tone was dry. 'Thank you. Last time

we met, you were not half so gallant, Señor
Castillo.'

His smooth brow creased in a frown. 'We have
met before? Surely not, I would have remembered
you very well.'

'Probably not,' Laura relented, smiling, 'considering I was ten years old and you were about
eight.'

'Ah, you remember coming to the Mexico City
house?' Isabel broke in delightedly. 'No wonder
you write so well, with such a memory!'

'But of course,' Nicolas put in as if just
reminded of her accomplishment, 'we are
honoured by the visit of a famous author.'

'Hardly that.' Laughing awkwardly, Laura was
relieved when Isabel instructed her son to bring
aperitifs before dinner.

'I would not like to upset the cook we have
now,' she explained as Nicolas went to the small
bar in the corner. 'Román himself found her, and
he would be furious if she complained to him
about our lateness.'

'My cousin,' remarked Nicolas in a reversion to
sourness as he came back bearing three small
glasses of pale sherry on a silver salver, 'seldom
eats with us, yet he scours the earth looking for a
cook who can cater to his exclusive tastes.'

There was a note of warning in Isabel's
'Nicolas!' and after a brief pursing of his full
young mouth, he turned on his charm again,
proving a witty and entertaining host there and
later in the almost oppressive heaviness of the
dining room across the hall. Later, Laura
reflected that without his sparkling company the
evening would have been unnaturally subdued

under the vengeful glares of portraited Castillos lining the high-ceilinged room. More than once she quivered as her eyes met the burning fierceness of a lean-jawed ancestor directly in her line of vision. It wouldn't have surprised her at all to find that Román Castillo himself had posed for the portrait.

The excellently cooked meal left only fleeting impressions of the bleached white of hearts of palm, succulent pork slices in a spicy sauce, a rich chocolate cake dessert which Isabel, eyeing ruefully, enjoyed guiltily.

'We'll take coffee in the *sala chica*,' she instructed the silently efficient maid at the end of the meal, rising and waiting for her son and Laura to accompany her back to the small salon which, together with the dining room, was all Laura had seen of the grandly historic house.

'If you will excuse me, Mamá, Laura,' Nicolas interrupted her thoughts, 'I must leave you now. There is someone I must see on a business matter.'

'Business!' Isabel remarked sourly as she watched her son's rapid stride to the rear of the hall. 'Who conducts business at this hour? Men!' she spat contemptuously, then forced a smile for Laura's benefit as she continued towards the small salon. 'My nephew, Román, also leaves us after the meal, but he at least makes no excuses about business. He credits me with enough intelligence to know that his business at night is concerned only with women.'

Laura blinked, more surprised by Isabel's lack of censure at her nephew's randy lifestyle than her displeasure at her son's departure. Isabel rallied, however, when coffee was brought to them in delicately fluted china cups, and prattled on happily about the house, which Laura would see in its entirety, she promised, the next day.

'The Villa Castillo has an interesting history,' she divulged. 'Don Salvador was the first Castillo to make his home here . . . naturally, since he was the one to have it built. It was to here that he brought his bride, Delfina, who was very beautiful. She was small and slender, with haunting dark eyes. You will see her portrait tomorrow, but of course it was painted when she came to the house as Don Salvador's bride, before the tragedies befell the young couple.'

'Tragedies?' Despite her afternoon rest, Laura had to force interest in what Isabel was saying. She felt desperately tired suddenly, perhaps the result of the long flight from New York that day. A vision of her compact apartment there flitted tantalisingly across her consciousness, and she wished with fierce nostalgia that she were there now, climbing into her own narrow bed to fall into the unconsciousness of sleep.

'Their first three children were lost before birth,' Isabel went on animatedly, 'so you can imagine their joy when the fourth, Luis, lived and grew to manhood. He, too, had just one son—oh, I am boring you, Laura,' she broke off contritely when Laura's heavy lids finally closed over the intense blue of her eyes.

'No, really,' she struggled to a straighter position in the comfortably padded armchair. 'It's just that—I guess I'm tired from the flight. Will you excuse me if I go to bed now?'

'Yes, of course. Our climate is almost perfect,

but our altitude has a tiring effect on people not used to it.'

Once more Laura was thankful to escape to the quiet of her room, hardly noticing the elaborately carved iron sconces set into the walls, lighting her way up the thickly carpeted staircase. Within minutes of laying her head on the plump feather pillows, she drifted off to sleep

CHAPTER TWO

LAURA'S sleep was dreamless and lasted until Rosa knocked tentatively on her door and came into the bedroom bearing a tray with a light breakfast arranged on it.

'Is it too early for you?' she asked tentatively, averting her eyes when Laura shot up in bed and groped for her watch, letting the covers slide down to the waist of her revealing pale blue nightdress.

'Heavens, no!' Peering at her watch, she saw that it registered nine. 'I don't usually sleep this late, and——' she pushed back her tousled hair and grinned at the maid, 'I don't usually have breakfast brought to me.'

'The Señora always has breakfast in her room,' Rosa explained shyly, seeming relieved when Laura fluffed up the pillows behind her and drew the sheet modestly up to her shoulders. Arranging the tray across Laura's knees, she went on, 'The Señora has asked me to give you her apologies. She had forgotten that she has an appointment this morning and she will not be able to show you the villa.'

'Oh.'

Laura's disappointment was so obvious that the maid hastened to reassure her. 'But the Señora says you are welcome to make the tour yourself, if you wish.'

'Oh, yes, I'd like that. Thank you, Rosa.'

Unable to resist the odour of fragrant coffee any longer, she poured from the large pot into the capacious breakfast cup.

'You take nothing in your coffee, *señorita*?'

Laura shook her head, and the maid retreated to the door. 'I will come back to fill your bath soon.'

'There's no need for that,' Laura quickly declined. 'I'll probably just have a shower for now.' She had no intentions of letting the maid spoil her to death for the short time she would be here . . . having her every whim fulfilled could become habit-forming, and her normal lifestyle just wouldn't support that kind of luxury.

Helping herself from the selection of pastries the kitchen had sent up for her breakfast, she reflected happily on the morning ahead. Isabel Castillo was a very warm, nice lady, but her constant chatter would distract Laura from her purpose. Later there would be time to fill in the historic facts of the mansion, but for now she just wanted to get the feel of it in her own wanderings.

Forty-five minutes later, showered and dressed in sunny yellow linen skirt and paler shirt-blouse, she decided to explore her own floor first, at least this side of it, before tackling the many rooms opening off the main hall below.

Passing by the heavy closed doors in her own corridor, which were obviously bedrooms—she had no desire to come across a still-sleeping Nicolas or a half-dressed Isabel—she walked up to where the hall widened for the staircase. Giving a precautionary tap on one half of the double doors to her right, she went into the dim

mustiness of a room that had obviously been
unused for years. Light crept feebly in at the
edge of the curtains covering a window opposite
and she felt strangely impelled to cross the room
and shed light on it. Blinking as she swept the
dusty curtains aside and daylight flooded that
section of the room, she turned and gasped as her
eyes took in its immensity, a size that not even
the plethora of massive Colonial furniture could
diminish.

Pride of place was taken by a huge, elaborately
canopied bed, its hangings and coverlet of the
royal purple and gold. Ancient armoires and
carved wood wardrobes gave an eerie splendour
to the room, as did the huge open fireplace of old
brick flanked by two spartan wooden armchairs
with stretched leather for seat and back. The
floor was of wood, dust obscuring its ancient
patina, with a scattering of rugs here and there,
their designs that had once been vividly coloured
now faded to drabness.

Laura shivered and moved back to replace the
curtains. The room wasn't scary in a ghostly
sense, just . . . *unhappy*, somehow. It needed little
imagination to know that this must have been the
master bedroom at one time, though it obviously
hadn't been used as that for a long, long time.
Why? she wondered as she unconsciously tiptoed
out and closed the door behind her with a sigh.
The unmarried Román had had no reason to use
it, but what of his parents? Or was that it? Had
his father closed off the room after his wife's
death?

Reminding herself that she was being un-
forgivably curious about the family's private

affairs, she went downstairs and spent an idyllic half hour investigating the lower floor apart from the kitchens and servants' quarters at the rear. Her imagination raced as she wandered from one room to another, each containing a fortune, she was sure, in antique furniture, exquisite glass and porcelain collections, and in the library expensively bound books reaching up towards the high ceiling. Her own parents were comfortably well off, but this was something else again. Happily, she recognised that it was all exactly the kind of setting she needed for her hero's background.

He would be carelessly arrogant about his wealth, never having known anything else. Women would be attracted helplessly to his dark, almost saturnine good looks, to his air of mastery, his control over all his affairs, business and personal. Such control had dictated his marriage to the unfortunate Maria Delgado, the only daughter of an industrial tycoon who had fallen in love with her husband shortly after the marriage. Laura yearned over her fictitious heroine's dilemma—should she remain as she was, lovingly pliable under his masterful dictates, or should she fight for her own individual place in the sun of his presence?

Almost oblivious of her surroundings, Laura thoughtfully mounted the right-hand staircase leading off the central hall. Her heroine, Maria, had latent spirit lurking underneath her shy acquiescence, so she would fight the boldly confident women in her husband's life. She would learn how to make the most of her good points, to develop a scintillating conversational style that would bind him, enthralled, to her side. . .

There was a different atmosphere in this side of the house, Laura decided, absorbing the air of tasteful elegance that met her in room after room. The furniture here was light-hearted, if elegant and sophisticated. A pleasant sitting room was filled with bright chintz and intricately carved French period pieces which contrasted sharply with the rest of the house. Whoever lived here had a delicious sense of humour, a puckishness that juxtaposed Meissen china treasures with humorously portrayed Mexican figures of fun. The last room she entered was sparsely furnished, the only note of extravagance a canopied bed of comfortable proportions covered with a scarlet and gold spread, colours which were echoed in the fulsome canopy and caught in the more subdued rugs scattered here and there over the softly gleaming wood floor.

Laura stepped across to the intricately carved writing desk situated to take the light from a high vaulted window close to the sleeping area, her fingers touching the silver candlesticks which were obviously more ornamental than useful. Her eyes fell on a letter opened for casual inspection, a letter that began: 'Román, *mi amor*. . .' Fastidiously, Laura ignored what was obviously a love letter, though her mind automatically translated fact into fiction. Maria could possibly discover a love letter to her husband from one of his *amores*. She would feel revulsion at first, then pique, then a newfound determination to bind her husband to her in more ways than the expedient or legal. The other women in his life

were boldly confident of their assets; then so
would she be.

'Is my personal correspondence of such great
interest to you, *señorita*, that you invade my
privacy to gain access to it?'

The softly menacing male voice, using English,
came from the doorway, and Laura automatically
looked down at the private correspondence in
question, inexplicably clasped tightly in one
hand, before looking up and sideways to the man
who had spoken. Her eyes opened wide when
they fell on the figure that had become so familiar
to her in dreams . . . the tall, expensively suited
man who stood there was the hero of her novel to
the last small detail. A thin, angular face topped
by blue-black hair cut in a studiedly casual style
that was neither long nor short, the haughty lift
of well-marked black eyebrows, the sardonic
twist of narrow lips, were all devastatingly
familiar to her.

'*You!*' she breathed, unable to take her eyes
from him, though a saner part of her whirling
brain told her that this was no fictional hero, that
she was no Maria Delgado plotting ways to
capture her husband's love.

She watched, fascinated, as the man walked
towards her and deepened the sarcastic twist of
his lips.

'I believe we have not met before, *señorita*,' he
said with the same contained menace of his first
statement. His eyes, dark to the point of
blackness, went over the bright red-gold of her
hair, the slenderness of her figure outlined in
yellow. 'I assure you, I would have remembered
you.'

Laura's mouth felt horribly dry, and she moistened her lips in a nervous gesture that seemed to fascinate him. 'I—er—no, we haven't met before, *señor*. I'm—here as the guest of your aunt, Señora Castillo.'

The well-defined brows arched fractionally. 'So? Tia Isabel made no mention of expecting a visitor—especially a *norteamericana* beauty such as yourself.' He paused and looked at her expectantly; Laura stared back, still disorientated to find that the man she had imagined really existed. 'You know my identity,' he said a shade impatiently, 'so may I be informed of yours?'

Blushing, and feeling foolish in the extreme, Laura explained, 'Your aunt and my mother were friends years ago in Mexico City—my father was American Vice-Consul at the time. My name is Laura Benson.'

'Ah.' Nodding, he rocked on his heels for a moment, staring so hard that she felt uncomfortable.

'I'm sorry, *señor*, if I seemed to be prying. Your aunt was going to show me around the villa this morning, but she had another engagement. She said it would be all right for me to—look around on my own.'

'You are interested in Colonial era houses?'

'Well, yes—you see, I'm——'

'Then you should have an informed guide when viewing this one,' he said abruptly, glancing at the slim-line watch fastened to one black-haired wrist. 'Come, I will give you a— what do you call it?—a mini-tour myself.' Turning, he added sarcastically, 'Most parts of the house are more interesting historically than these quarters of mine.'

Laura hastened to catch up with his impatiently rapid stride, coming abreast with him at the still-open door. Taking advantage of his courteous gesture of standing aside to let her pass, she tried again in a voice thick with embarrassment.

'I assure you, Señor Castillo, that I had no intention of spying on your personal life by coming into your private quarters. I'd no idea whose rooms these were, because I was thinking of something entirely different. You see, I——'

'No need to apologise, *señorita*,' he interrupted smoothly, sending a small electric shock along her arm when he took her elbow and led her out into the upper hall, drawing her attention to the intricately carved chests and chairs spaced around its perimeter. 'Now here we have excellent examples of the first Spanish influence on native Indian furniture. The carving is a blend of old and new cultures. Nowadays, of course, we prefer more comfort in our furnishings, so that reproductions of the originals are now padded to modern tastes, although the basic carving skills have been retained. This chair, for instance, served my ancestors well, but my own twentieth-century bones reject its discomforts while still prizing its elegant simplicity of design. This bench seat has an interesting history. . .'

His impersonal enthusiasm and expert recital of his home's treasures soon made Laura forget her former embarrassment, and she hung on his every comment, wishing desperately that she had thought to bring a notebook and pen. She would never remember all the fascinating details which could well be incorporated into her book. It was only when they entered the lofty dining room with its ancestral portraits that she was reminded of her initial shock on meeting him. Pausing before the likeness that had met her eye several times at dinner the night before, she knew that her instinct had been correct. Román Castillo, the man by her side, could well have posed for it. The same thinly arrogant features were outlined by the same dark eyebrows, the same thick black hair which in the portrait was styled a little longer.

'This could be a portrait of you,' she murmured, half to herself, and heard him chuckle, obviously amused by her comparison.

'I'm not sure if I should be flattered or offended,' he rejoined on a more human note than he had displayed so far, his tautly held lips relaxing over very white, very even teeth. 'I am his namesake, but there the resemblance ends, I hope. Don Román was married to a very beautiful lady who unfortunately for her was not content with only her husband's adoration. She suffered from what we would call in these days nymphomania, an endless need for men other than her husband, and Don Román was forced to take steps to curb her wandering affections.'

'Steps?' Laura asked faintly.

Román shrugged negligently. 'It would no doubt be considered barbaric now, but he kept her confined in their bedroom isolated from temptation for the last thirty years of their marriage.'

Laura's mouth dropped open in astonishment as she turned from the original to the too-lifelike replica, a shiver tingling down her back. 'That is barbaric,' she managed to say, the instant thought flashing through her mind that the closed room she had penetrated first on her tour could possibly be the one where Don Román had imprisoned his flighty wife. There had been that atmosphere of unhappiness, she had felt it clearly.

'To us, yes,' he answered easily, 'but in his mind he was justified. An unfaithful wife makes a comic figure of the man concerned, and the Castillo men have never been known for their tolerance of humiliation.'

'Is that why you've never taken the step of marriage?' she blurted out with unthinking rudeness, and saw his features tighten forbiddingly. What had possessed her to ask that tactless question of a man who so obviously prized his privacy? She was back to feelings of hot embarrassment that sent waves of deepening colour into her cheeks.

But his reply was mild, considering the fiery blast she had expected. 'I have never anticipated humiliation in marriage,' he said smoothly, his black eyes glittering in the light from the long, narrow window next to them.

His obvious meaning only served to deepen her embarrassment, and she turned away, relieved to hear sounds of Isabel's return in the hall. Would he now make his displeasure known at having had a brash North American visitor foisted on him? She could hardly blame him. An aristocrat in his part of the world, a world that took for granted the more favoured status of male over female— she must seem brash to him.

Her chin went up as she went towards the hall, sensing that he followed her at a slower pace

Perhaps she had been more forward than his Latin tastes admired, but what was that to her? She was a product of the modern age in a country that had taken the long road to women's emancipation from such tyrannous bonds. Just because she was unwillingly indebted to him for a temporary roof over her head there was no reason to slough off her deeply felt independence.

'Ah, Laura,' Isabel greeted her in the hall, her tweed-encased figure obviously feeling the effects of the day's warmth, 'you have been finding your way round, I see. I am so sorry that I forgot my appointment this morning, but——' Her eyes went over Laura's shoulder and widened into momentary panic. 'Román! I had no idea that you were coming home today! If so, I would certainly have cancelled my appointment and been here to greet you.'

'It would have been unnecessary,' he responded in Spanish, giving his aunt a perfunctory kiss of greeting. 'Your—guest has been interesting company for me.'

Isabel cast a nervous look at Laura's heightened colour and taut lips, and drew her own conclusions. 'I should have told you about her visit,' she said in rapid Spanish, her eyes darting back to Román, 'but there seemed no chance before you went to Mexico——'

'There's no need to apologise on my behalf,' Laura inserted crisply in the same language, and felt Román Castillo's stare fasten on her pink cheeks. 'If my visit is an inconvenience to Señor Castillo, I can easily move to a hotel until my research is completed.'

'Research?' he murmured, evidently surprised on two counts, and Laura knew that she should have made her familiarity with Spanish known to him . . . it just hadn't occurred to her, his English was so flawless.

'Did Laura not tell you?' Isabel cried traitorously. 'She is a famous author, and she came here to do research for her second book.'

The black brows rose with insulting question. 'Fame on the strength of one book? You must indeed have an extraordinary talent, Miss Benson!' His use of English made the remark more insulting than it might have been.

'I was fortunate enough to receive favourable book reviews,' she said distantly, 'but fame is very short-lived in the literary world. This week's wonder is next week's has-been.'

'Modesty becomes you, Miss Benson,' he retorted evenly, 'but it should not be taken too far. Far from inconveniencing me, your visit in my home is an honour I do not take lightly. Please permit me to offer my help in any way I can in your research.' His courtly bow from the waist would have seemed effeminate in an American man, but in him it was entirely graceful, if performed tongue in cheek. 'I trust my aunt has given you suitable quarters?'

Isabel jumped in before Laura could form a reply. 'I've put Laura in the Don Felipe room, and provided her with a desk and chair for her work.'

He nodded gravely. 'Excellent. She will not be disturbed at the end of the corridor, even Nicolas will——' his gaze narrowed and directed itself to the hall's left-hand stairway. 'Has he been attending to the business I left with him?' he asked abruptly.

Isabel looked decidedly shifty, but staunchly defended her only child. 'He has been working late on business—only last night, he left us after dinner to conduct more of it. Is that not so, Laura?' she appealed to the younger woman, who resented being brought in as a doting mother's ally.

'He left us after dinner, yes,' she said carefully, refusing to meet Román's sharpened gaze, 'saying that he had business to take care of.'

'You see?' Isabel cried triumphantly. 'Nicolas is as conscientious when you are away as when you are here. Why——'

'Where is he now?' Román interrupted brusquely.

'Nicolas? Why, he is—I'm sure he is working hard in the office,' averred Isabel, betraying her own doubts as she glanced at the left staircase. 'I'm sure he must be, although he worked very late last night. It was two or three in the morning before he returned to the house, so——'

'If you'll excuse me, I'll——' Laura began, wishing to extricate herself from what was rapidly becoming a family squabble, only to hear the object of the exercise say sleepily from the top of the stairs.

'Mamá, why didn't you tell Rosa to bring my coffee at noon? You know I always have——' His sleep-drowsed eyes shot open when he focused clearly on the trio in the hall below, his olive skin paling to a sickly cream when he took in the fact that it was indeed his cousin, Román, who formed one third of it. For long moments he stared speechlessly down into his cousin's grim expression, then rallied with an admirable force of will. 'Román! How nice to see you back! But we hadn't expected you to be finished with your business in Mexico City so soon!'

'That much is obvious,' Román responded drily, drawing Laura's eyes to the whitely taut lines of anger round his arrogant mouth. For a moment she felt sympathy for the younger man, although it was only too obvious that he was more of a liability than asset to the family business concerns. With a flick of his immaculately pressed shirt cuff, he glanced at his watch. 'I will expect a full report from you on your negotiations with the Garcia Company when I return to the office at three-thirty after lunch with the State Governor. Make sure everything is in order, cousin, or I might be forced to make decisions painful for both of us.' He turned away, but Isabel's breathless pleading brought his head round, his eyes blankly neutral as they met her agitated gaze.

'Your father would not have been so hard on a kinsman,' she faltered emotionally.

Román said nothing for a moment, his eyes sparking a deep anger that made Laura forget her virtual position as eavesdropper on close family matters.

At last he said heavily, 'It would perhaps have been better for Nicolas if he had been so with his father.' As Isabel caught her breath noisily, he turned coldly away and said over his shoulder, 'I will be dining out tonight, but please arrange a formal meal for tomorrow night, when I have a guest.'

He completely ignored Laura on his march from the hall to the outside world, but she preferred it that way. Inside, she was trembling more than Isabel showed outwardly because family squabbles were alien to her, particularly when strangers were present. The Castillos evidently had no such reticence, and she stared in amazement as Isabel spiked on her high-heeled shoes across the hall to the small salon, unperturbed by the scene that had taken place.

'Let's have a drink before lunch,' she said in a relieved tone, moving to pour the drink herself from the bar behind the door. 'I need something strong—what about you?'

'White wine is fine for me,' Laura returned dazedly, watching as the older woman poured herself a generous portion of Scotch and sprayed it briefly with soda water.

'That's better,' she said heartily, sipping on her drink before carrying Laura's across to the chair where she had seated herself. 'Román is always a little touchy when he gets back from a business trip,' she confided, dropping into the sofa corner closest to Laura. 'He has a wonderful head for business, but it irritates him at the same time, and usually,' she sighed, gulping at the glass in her hand, 'poor Nico has to take the brunt of it.'

Poor Nico, nothing, Laura thought dispassionately, tasting the tart yet sweet white wine. The most lenient boss in the world wouldn't put up with slothful work habits, and something told her that Román Castillo would demand and expect even more from a relative than from the faceless hordes he must employ. The same instinct told her that he would be no less demanding of himself . . . what was this? Was she defending the man who stood for everything she hoped to denigrate in her novel? Remorselessly confident in his own abilities, expecting even his wife to conform to his autocratic way of life?

'It must be a woman he has asked to have dinner with us tomorrow,' Isabel conjectured moodily, draining her glass and popping up to refill it. 'Probably Mercedes Ortez has followed him here from Mexico, or most likely travelled back with him in his private plane,' she ended viciously, settling herself again on the sofa, frowning into her glass.

'Is she his fiancée?' asked Laura, surprised by the pang of disappointment that shot through her.

'She would like to be, of course—many women would like to become the wealthy Don Román's wife,' Isabel's voice was tinged with contempt, 'but he is not easily fooled by women's ambitious ways.'

'Wouldn't he have brought her here to stay if she returned from the city with him?' Laura soothed. 'Perhaps as he asked for a formal dinner it's a business acquaintance he wants to entertain.'

'Business, pah! Román keeps his home strictly apart from his business interests. No, I am sure the guest will be Mercedes Ortez.' Isabel looked up sharply at Laura. 'You have heard of her, of course.'

'No, I'm afraid I haven't.'

'No?' The older woman seemed astonished by this. 'She is very famous here in Mexico, mostly because of her television show, *An Hour with*

Mercedes. She interviews the rich and famous in our country, also visiting celebrities from other places.' Her eyes widened as she gazed at Laura. 'You would be perfect for her programme; speaking Spanish as you do, there would be no need for a translator.'

'Oh no, please,' protested Laura, seeing her peaceful anonymity shattered as it had been in the States, disrupting the quietude she needed to work on her new book. 'I'm really not much good at television interviews.'

'We shall see.'

The tap of hurrying heels sounded from the hall, and Isabel jumped up, running to intercept her son's belated departure for work.

'Nico! You must eat something before you leave, I insist!'

'There is no time, Mamá,' he returned irritably. 'Román's spies will tell him the exact moment I enter the office, and I have no wish to antagonise him further, or give him any excuse for getting rid of me.'

'As if he would do that to a member of the family! Nico, listen to——'

Moments later Isabel returned to the salon, frowningly disgruntled, and subjected Laura to an unwelcome harangue about Román, not her dilatory son.

When she paused for breath, Laura put in levelly, 'I really don't think I should concern myself with family matters, *señora*. As a guest in the house——'

'You are like the daughter I never had,' Isabel interrupted dramatically, 'and so you are like family to me. How often have I longed for a daughter to confide in, to have her confide in me!'

The appeal was hard to resist, but Laura had no desire to be caught up in the centre of this volatile family, to take sides in their seemingly frequent quarrels—besides, she already had a mother who suited her perfectly. Eleanor breezily went about her own business and made no demands on Laura for girlish confidences, though she was always open to the problems Laura needed help with.

Isabel had no such reticence, and questioned her relentlessly all through lunch, the *comida* which started at two and went on with interminable slowness.

'With such beauty, you must have many men wanting to marry you,' she said eagerly as Rosa served a delicious vegetable soup in pottery bowls. 'And after all, you must be—what? Twenty-one?'

'Almost twenty-three,' Laura picked up her spoon calmly, lifting her brows questioningly when Isabel choked on her first mouthful.

'Twenty-three?' she gasped, reaching desperately for the glass of white wine to the right of her plate and gulping rapidly. 'My dear, what happened?'

'Happened?'

'There must have been a tragic love affair for you to still be unmarried at this great age! Tell me about it, my dear.'

Feeling distinctly old-maidish, Laura wondered wryly if Gavin Foster would qualify as a 'tragic love affair'. Among the men she had dated for longer or shorter periods, a British diplomat, he stood out as the one who had affected her most. In Bonn three years ago when they met, she had ignored the fifteen years difference in their ages and fallen madly in love with his leanly handsome good looks, understated elegance, wordly ease—it had been impossible to ignore, however, the wife who had elected to stay in England with their three school-age sons. Gavin had mentioned divorce, but neither of them had wanted that kind of finality—perhaps they were both in love with the idea of being in love, she with a sophisticated older man, he with a naïve younger woman. They had parted without rancour on either side, were still friends who kept in touch occasionally.

'There was someone,' she satisfied Isabel's avid curiosity, 'but it wasn't possible for us to marry.'

The bright eyes widened in sympathetic question. 'He died?' breathed Isabel.

'He went back to his wife,' Laura stated bluntly, and was faintly irritated by the other woman's shocked intake of breath. The reaction might have been appropriate fifty years ago, even thirty, but today it was definitely out of place.

'You had an affair with a *married* man?' Isabel compounded the archaic implication.

'We didn't live together, if that's what you mean. We simply decided that neither of us wanted the mess of a divorce.'

'Div——?' Isabel seemed incapable of completing the word, but she rallied quickly and said, 'My poor child, you needed a mother's guidance, but her place has always been with your father, naturally. From now on, I want you to look on me as a substitute mother, one who will do her duty by you. The first thing is to find you a suitable husband—what you have just confided in me is between ourselves, you understand. No man of pride would want a—how do you say it, a *left-over* for his bride. Now let me see. . .'

Exasperated, Laura watched her hostess turn over the possibilities in her mind. 'Please don't bother, *señora*,' she said crisply. 'I've no wish to marry right now, here or anywhere else.'

'Mmm?' the older woman queried with maddening distraction. 'Of course every girl wants to marry, Laura. You've just been hurt by this—this devil of a married man! Don't worry, I'll find you a *novio* who has no such entanglements. Yes, Rosa,' she addressed the maid who had brought in the next course, 'you may take the soup away, I've let it go cold.'

The situation would have been comical had it not been so irritating, Laura thought as she helped herself to the fish main dish and vegetables that accompanied it. What would it take to convince the Señora that she was perfectly satisfied with her single state? One day she would like to marry, have children, make a home for them, but that time was not yet. When it came, the choice would be her own, not calculating machinations of a repressed matron! The thought had merit only insofar as it would occupy Isabel's seemingly fertile imagination and frustrated mother instinct and so give herself time to complete the work she had come here to do.

Her enjoyment of the meal would have been more than a little marred had she known the direction Isabel's thoughts had taken. As it was, she silently congratulated the cook, Román's 'find', on the excellence of the food. The delicate flavour of the white fish was balanced by a tangy sauce, and the vegetables were crisp without being underdone. The custard dessert that followed was light and creamy, the coffee brewed to perfection when it appeared.

Isabel's suggestion that they rest for a while after the meal met with her hearty approval. For the first time, she saw sense in the Mexican tradition of an afternoon siesta.

CHAPTER THREE

LAURA gazed critically at herself in the full-length mirror situated between the closet doors, smoothing the soft folds of white silk skirt over her hips at the same time as her eyes went up to the revealing bodice topping it. Gentle swirls of white silk draped from her shoulders and sparsely down over her breasts, to be caught in at the waist in a much-folded cummerbund effect.

'Wear your most beautiful dress,' Isabel had advised, an innocent gleam in her dark eyes. The prompting had come only minutes after viewing the voluptuously beautiful Mercedes Ortez conducting her weekly programme, broadcast the night before. The Mexican woman's breathtaking beauty had come across vibrantly on the small screen as she interviewed a trio of comedians and a contrastingly sober economist ... even his lugubrious features had relaxed under the effects of her flatteringly deferential smile, which lit up the velvet softness of her dark eyes. Who could blame Román Castillo if he were more than a little in love with the enchanting hostess of a widely watched talk show? Any man would be proud to acknowledge her as his girl-friend, fiancée, *wife*.

The last category brought a knife-like pain to Laura's middle, one she dismissed as being ridiculous in the extreme. She had only met the man once, for heaven's sake! And that meeting had been fraught with embarrassment after he had discovered her in his private quarters, seemingly snooping through his equally private correspondence.

'Come in,' she said abstractedly when a light tap sounded at the door, and Isabel entered, her eyes widening in bright admiration when she saw the cool elegance of Laura's dress.

'It is perfect!' she exclaimed, clasping her hands rapturously. 'Román will not be able to take his eyes from you!'

'Román?' murmured Laura, still not sure that the dress was appropriate for the studied dignity of the Castillo dining room.

'But of course. He has an eye for a beautiful woman, that one.'

Laura gave her a dry smile. 'That's obvious in his choice of dinner partner,' she pointed out. 'I'm really not out to impress Román or any other man tonight.' The last she added in case Isabel was habouring any wild ideas of pairing her off for life with her precious, and spoiled, son. That really would be a fate worse than death!

'But you will make a strong impression,' the older woman stated triumphantly, 'and it is perhaps better if you remain as cool as you are now. Nothing puts a man off more than a woman too anxious to please him—that has been Román's trouble for too long, if only his women friends knew it!' She rushed back to the door before Laura had time to voice the horrified conviction that had just come to her. 'We must hurry in order to be here when they arrive. Román left thirty minutes ago to collect

Mercedes, and I want him to see you first as being perfectly at home in his house, a beautiful hostess.'

Laura had to hurry to catch up with her flying figure along the corridor. A sudden flare of temper brought a deepening of the light blusher she had applied to her cheeks, and at the top of the stairs she hissed.

'*Señora*, will you please stop this! Can't you understand that I'm not even remotely interested in your nephew, as a husband or anything else! I——' Halfway down the stairs, she stopped abruptly when the heavy front door opened suddenly, the rest of the words frozen in her throat as she watched Román usher in the beautiful young Mexican woman she had watched on television the night before. In person, she was even more breathtaking than in her small screen image, a long, full-skirted yellow dress pointing up the vivid darkness of her black hair, arranged in a cloud around her piquantly animated face as she laughed up into Román's eyes.

Laura gripped the stair rail with one hand, unable to pull her eyes away as Román made a murmured remark and slid the floor-length black velvet cloak from the other girl's shoulders. Unaware of her own unusual beauty, she was still paralysed on the spot when Román led his dinner guest across the hall in the direction of the larger *sala* next to the dining room. As if sensing that she and Isabel, who had also remained still on the stairs, were there, he turned his head and raised his eyes at the last moment.

His aunt received a cursory inspection, but on Laura's face and figure he lingered. When their eyes met, it was as if electric voltage shot through her. If she hadn't suspected otherwise, she would have thought the stunned awareness in his gaze held an element of shyness.

It was Mercedes who broke up the tableau-like numbness. Her eyes following Román's, she smiled sunnily and said, 'Tia Isabel! It's been so long since we met.'

Animated into motion, Isabel tripped down the rest of the stairs and went regally to greet their guest, enfolding her in what Laura thought sourly was a hypocritical hug, considering her constant denigration of the television star.

'We must lay the blame on you for that, *cariña*,' Isabel said sweetly. 'You live such an exciting life in Mexico that you forget your old friends! And who can blame you? Even an old lady like me might be tempted by the attentions of all the rich and handsome men who must flock round you there.'

Laura, going hesitantly towards the group, saw the dark girl give Román a raised brow glance, to which he shook his head faintly, as if reassuring her that his aunt's insinuation meant nothing to him. There was such an easy familiarity between the three of them that Laura wished she had the fortitude to turn her back on them and return to her room. Isabel, however, had no intention of letting her escape so easily.

'Ah, here you are, Laura. Come and meet our celebrity—but I'm forgetting. Laura is also a famous person,' she informed the politely smiling Mercedes.

'So I have heard from Román,' Mercedes allowed her smile to deepen, showing the white

perfection of her evenly shaped teeth. 'I am
envious of your talent, *señorita*.'

Even the most suspicious character could not
have found anything but genuine admiration in
the dark girl's sparkling eyes, and Laura warmed
to her.

'You have no need to envy anyone,' she
returned, stretching out her hand to clasp the
other woman's hand. 'Millions of people must
envy you your talent. I'm Laura Benson.'

'I'm not—or shouldn't be—envied for the
reason Tia Isabel has given,' laughed Mercedes.
'Most men are terrified of successful women.'
Her upward glance at Román stated that he could
not be numbered among them, a surprising
revelation to Laura. Her guess would have been
that the autocratic Don Román had to resent any
kind of superior talent in a woman.

'Why are we standing here in the hall when we
could be enjoying drinks at the fire?' he closed
the subject, shepherding the women into the
cavernous large salon where a fire did, indeed,
crackle happily in the massive grate. Manuel,
who evidently doubled as butler for the household, took their orders for pre-dinner drinks and
went quietly from the room.

'You speak excellent Spanish, Señorita
Benson,' Mercedes remarked, taking her place at
Román's side on one of the Louis XVI sofas
flanking the fireplace, her skirt spreading to
partially cover one taut, black-clad thigh. Like
maiden aunt and spinster cousin, Isabel and
Laura took the other.

'That's because——'

'I was telling her exactly the same thing last

night,' Isabel broke in excitedly. 'She would be excellent for your show, Mercedes, do you not think so? As I told her, the publicity would be good for her sales here in Mexico—don't you agree?'

'I was about to suggest the same thing myself,' Mercedes replied with a hint of dryness before turning to look fully at Laura. 'It could be good for both of us if you would appear on my show. I lose so many interviews because of the language difficulty, and your sales would possibly increase in this country. Especially as you have come here to research the background for your second novel.'

'Exactly what I said to her,' Isabel leaned forward eagerly. 'It would be like—what is it called?—advance publicity!'

'Why not let Miss Benson decide for herself what she would like to do for publicity?' Román put in with sarcastic dryness, and Laura flashed him a grateful look.

'I'd really like to get on with the research for the moment. Perhaps later, before I go back to the States?' she appealed to Mercedes, who smiled and nodded agreeably.

'We could tape the interview at any time,' she said, 'and release it just before you leave, or after if you prefer.'

The subject was dropped, and Nicolas created a stir with his belated arrival, which coincided with Manuel's re-entry with the drinks.

'I'm sorry to be late, but,' the younger man glanced at his cousin seated completely at his ease among the ladies, 'my talks with Felipe Garcia took longer than expected. But I laid out our terms for the contract, and he——'

'Let's leave business until tomorrow,' suggested Román, a steely note in his voice. 'Bring Señor Nicolas whatever he wants to drink,' he instructed the waiting Manuel, 'and then we can eat. I'm starving!'

'I thought I would change first,' said Nicolas with tentative stubbornness, and was immediately overruled.

'You look suitably dressed to me,' Román said with a flick of his black eyes over his cousin's dark business suit, going on with a trace of irritation, 'Tell Manuel what you want and we can continue with our dinner party.'

Nicolas flushed under his olive tan and curtly ordered his drink, but that was the extent of his display of anger at his cousin's imperious manner. He dropped into one of the armchairs facing the fireside group and held a moody silence, while Laura seethed on his behalf. There had been absolutely no need for Román to flex his head-of-the-family muscles. True, he had caught Nicolas lazing the day away on his arrival home that morning, but it was obvious the younger man had stretched himself since then to generate company business—to be greeted by the quiet contempt some dog owners used on their unwilling charges.

Other than make a scene, she had no choice but to take the arm Román proffered, the other taken willingly by his aunt, on their way in to dinner. Nicolas, making no effort to hide his admiration, followed with Mercedes. But of course Román had no fears of losing his lover to the younger man . . . as opposed to Nicolas, and most others who would aspire to her beauty and charm, he had the confidence of stature, wealth, and an aristocratic background few of his compatriots shared. An ordinary mortal didn't stand a chance against him. And apart from all that, he possessed the dark good looks women had lusted after through the ages. To her dismay, Laura found herself seated next to him—naturally, on his right!—at the long dining table more suited for twenty than for five. Isabel presided in the hostess's position at the other end, while Mercedes and Nicolas faced each other across the centre. General conversation was restricted, and soon two sets of private communication were under way, Isabel not seeming to mind her isolation in solitary state as she beamed short-sightedly down the table.

'Tell me about your new book, Miss—may I call you Laura? It seems foolish to cling to formality when we are to be so closely connected for—how long will your research take? A week, a month, a year?'

Laura gave him a frosty look. 'I wouldn't dream of inconveniencing you for as long as a year, Señor Castillo. I hope I'll be finished inside a month.'

'I have already told you that your presence in my home is an honour, not an inconvenience,' he said coolly, acknowledging the soup Manuel placed before him with a slight nod. 'And I would prefer it if you would call me Román.'

'As you like,' Laura returned ungraciously, lifting her spoon to attack the soup and noticing that Román, despite his hunger, had waited until she did so before lifting his own. Irritably, she asked, 'Why were you named Román instead of the more usual Ramón?'

He shrugged. 'A family tradition. There have been four Don Románs during the past two hundred years, including myself.' He slanted her a sharply penetrating look and she dropped her gaze to the hearty soup before her. 'Is it my name that troubles you, Laura, or is there perhaps another reason for your disapproval of me?'

'I—don't know what you mean.'

'I mean,' he sounded amused, yet exasperated, 'that you have been giving me what you call, I believe, the cold shoulder. Have I offended you in some way unknown to me?'

'No, of course not.' The words sounded unconvincing even to her own ears, and Román picked up on it.

'Come now, Laura, I am not completely insensitive to a woman's moods! Tell me what it is that troubles you.'

'If you really want to know,' she retorted coldly, 'I think you treat Nicolas very badly.'

'Oh?'

'Yes,' she rushed on. 'Maybe he's not the best timekeeper in the world, but shouldn't you, as head of the family business, encourage him when he shows signs of diligence?'

His black brows rose laconically. 'Has he done that?'

'You know he has!' she shot back furiously, abandoning interest in her soup as she faced him squarely. 'Tonight, for instance, when he tried to tell you of his successful meeting with—with Garcia or whoever, you acted as if it wasn't important and put him down in an embarrassing way. I've always thought encouragement shows more results than constant criticism.'

Expecting a well-directed barrage, she bent her head towards her plate and waited for it. But again he surprised her with the mildness of his reply.

'And I have always thought that business would be confined to the office, and not brought into the home.' He paused and, sensing that he had something further to say, Laura lifted her head and looked at him, surprising a speculatively amused glint in his black eyes. 'You have the instincts of a mother, Laura, but are you being protective of my cousin for other reasons? For instance,' he quoted her own mode of expression back to her, 'a romantic indulgence? I assure you that much though Nicolas would enjoy being handed from one over-protective mother to another, he is not the man for you.' Ignoring Laura's indignant gasp, he went on thoughtfully, 'No, I think you need a masterful hand yourself. Such pride and spirit demands an inflexible hand on the reins of marriage.'

Was he playing with her, inciting the swift anger that did indeed sparkle in the deep blue of her eyes? She felt the white heat of it, the warm spots of colour on each cheek, but still she went recklessly ahead.

'Meaning yours, *señor*?'

Their eyes locked in challenge, fierce blue, glittering black.

'Perhaps, Laura,' he murmured, 'perhaps.'

The rush of warmth to her limbs was the last thing she expected, and she was relieved when Mercedes lifted her voice to include them in the badinage she had been exchanging with Nicolas, though she shook so much that she scarcely heard the ensuing general conversation. This trembling awareness of the man beside her was a facet of romantic girlhood she had thought was left behind with high school days. Then, the newness of sexual awakening and its overtones were quite acceptable; now, a poised young woman of what she had fondly imagined were coolly sophisticated looks was shaking like green aspen leaf because a poised, confident and darkly good-looking Latin had joked about marriage with her.

'What has Román been saying to you, Laura?' Mercedes queried with a lightness that might have concealed deeper and more disturbing thoughts. 'You have not been listening to one word of our conversation.'

'I—I'm sorry, I guess I was thinking of something else,' Laura said quickly, hoping the beautiful Mercedes hadn't the ability to read thoughts and feelings.

'Ah,' she said with an understanding twinkle, 'you writers are all the same, always thinking of your work. Are we allowed to ask what the new book is about? I know,' she turned with a laugh to the rest of the table, 'how temperamental authors can be about works in progress. Only a few weeks ago I interviewed a scientist who was writing a very deep treatise on the effects of a newly discovered electro-magnetic ray, and he absolutely refused to discuss it. As if I or any of my viewing audience would have understood a word of it anyway!' Her gurgle of laughter was infectious, and the group around the table laughed with her.

'He probably had hopes of reaching the best-seller lists with it,' Román capped with dry

humour, and the conversation became general, to
Laura's heartfelt relief. How could she expound
on her new novel when the chief character was an
almost exact replica of their host? True, he had
no marriage-of-convenience wife pining for his
love, but the beautiful Mercedes obviously
expected to become his wife, which would
amount to the same thing in the end. It was only
too easy to imagine his murmured approaches to
other women, marriage being no obstacle.

Coffee was served in the large salon, and they
seated themselves like automatons as before.
Laura despised herself for noticing that Mercedes'
filmy skirt occupied a larger than ever portion of
Román's dark-clad thigh, and castigated herself
for being thoroughly unreasonable. What could
be more natural than the physical closeness of
two people who intended to marry?

She shouldn't have accepted the liqueur
offered with coffee. Her brain was already fogged
with the pre-dinner drink, the wine with the
meal, but she nodded recklessly when Manuel
brought a tray of mixed liqueurs, pointing to the
Mexican one that went so well with coffee.

'I must shop for some clothes tomorrow,'
Isabel unintentionally diverted the subject from
Laura's new book, 'would you care to join me,
Laura?'

'More clothes, Aunt?' Román inserted on a dry
note before Laura could respond. 'The Empress
Carlotta's wardrobe would have dimmed to
insignificance compared to yours!'

Irritated, Isabel ran a hand over the basic black
that was the stable of many women's wardrobes.
'I need at least two more dinner dresses, and

Laura will no doubt like to buy some pretty things.'

'What she is wearing looks—very becoming to me,' he let his dark eyes wander deliberately over the dress in question, as if he had a proprietorial right to do so. 'What exactly are you plotting for our lovely guest?' he switched his shrewd gaze to his aunt, who grew faintly pink.

'What should I be plotting, except that she should enjoy her visit to Guadalajara as much as possible?' She gave her nephew a tight little smile. 'As you have said yourself, she is a very lovely young woman, and I would like to introduce her to my friends.'

His lids narrowed in amusement. 'Particularly the ones with eligible sons?' he suggested drily, turning his head to Laura again. 'You must be wary of my aunt, Laura, she is the city's number one matchmaker. Before you know it, you will be shopping for a wedding dress and your career as a writer will be over.'

Mercedes, who had been a silent spectator until now, gave a gentle but noticeable hoot of derision. 'Ah, Román, how your shoulders must ache from carrying all those outdated traditions! Why should Laura give up her career just because she takes a husband? I certainly have no intention of doing so!'

Román's frown seemed significant to Laura, but his tone was quietly even when he said, 'Perhaps you will yet change your mind, *chica*.'

The emphasis had changed once again from Laura's affairs, and for that she was thankful. But the time to nip Isabel's ambitions for her in the bud was right now. She drew a deep breath.

'Many thanks, *señora*,' she addressed Isabel, 'but I must concentrate on the work I came here to do. I'm afraid I have a one-track mind where that's concerned, so——'

'I had not intended to take up all of your time,' Isabel broke in with hurt dignity, 'but not even Román works twenty-four hours a day! It is important to relax too, and forget the things that worry us for a little while—especially,' she lowered her voice to a stage whisper which could be heard in the far corners of the room, 'past troubles.'

So much for the older woman treating her confidence about Gavin as 'between you and me', Laura thought wryly, the implication being quite clear that 'past troubles' referred to romantic liaisons. But probably she was imagining the sharpened quality of Román's gaze, the widening of Mercedes' eyes in curious interest. They were too deeply embroiled in their own liaison to be bothered by hers! Suddenly she felt bone weary—a combined result of the alcohol she had consumed and the Guadalajara climate.

'If you'll excuse me,' she said, rising, 'I'm terribly tired. Would you mind if I retire now?'

Both Nicolas and Román rose politely. 'Our altitude takes time to become accustomed to,' the elder cousin agreed. 'Sleep well, Laura.'

His eyes were blandly courteous in the way of a good host's, and Laura thanked him before making her good night general. Her brain seemed stuffed with cotton wool as she made her way up the half-circle of the staircase, and she decided it would be wiser to use discretion in accepting alcoholic beverages, at least until her body had adjusted to the rarified atmosphere of Mexico's central plateau.

Despite her tiredness, Laura spent what seemed hours tossing and turning on her bed before finally throwing back the light covers and reaching for the negligee that matched the soft blue of her nightdress.

Quietly opening the balcony doors, she stepped out on to the tiled flooring and went to stand against the wrought iron railing enclosing it. The tall windows facing on to the courtyard gardens were in darkness, even those of Román opposite her own. Possibly, she conjectured drily, he had still been angry about Mercedes' refusal to give up her career after marriage and had dropped her off at her parents' house without lingering. In one way it had surprised her to learn that the vivaciously beautiful Mexican girl had lived in Guadalajara all her life; she seemed such a product of a cosmopolitan city like Mexico. On the other hand, what could be more natural than two offshoots of wealthy Guadalajaran society joining in marriage?

She smiled a little to herself. Román, like her hero, would think nothing of marrying expeditiously. He was that kind of man, unusual in these days, who clung tenaciously to the traditions of his forebears, and their marriages had been arranged without consulting the immediate parties. Love probably wouldn't enter into his decision when he finally decided the time was right to take a wife. It was also only too probable that he didn't know the meaning of love ... physical passion, yes, he had probably indulged

that aspect of his nature indiscriminately since
boyhood.

Indiscriminately? No, he would be choosy about
the women he associated with. Masterful, sar-
donically amused by the ease of the whole thing,
and—very exciting to the women he made love to.

The involuntary thought caught her unawares,
and she turned restlessly away from the balcony
and decided to take a walk in the courtyard
garden below. The moon would provide enough
light to see her way, and the household was
asleep so she would be completely alone with her
thoughts. The more she saw of Román Castillo
the clearer her fictional hero became, and she
wanted to pin down her impressions while they
were fresh in her mind.

Downstairs, she flitted like a ghost to the large
sliding doors leading to a covered terrace that
gave on to the garden. Stepping out, she saw that
here where it was darkest small lamps of exquisite
wrought iron were spaced at intervals against the
pillars supporting the heavy overhang. Interested,
she looked around at what was virtually an
outdoor living room with its thick tropical
greenery in massive pots of clay interspersed
between seating areas of round leather-topped
tables and tub chairs. On her right, a long,
narrow table of wood and patterned tile top was
obviously used for dining outdoors, seating
provided by high-backed chairs tucked neatly
under each side. It must be pleasant to eat out
here in the shade, she thought, when the really
hot weather came, and she felt a pang of what was
almost envy for the fortunate people who could
indulge such a lifestyle.

The thought brought her back to her hero and the characters rapidly taking form in her head, and she strolled on to the even lusher greenery of the gardens. The vividly hued geraniums in pots and beds, which she glimpsed from her windows, were only a little less spectacular in the cooler light of the moon. Following the closest path down the centre of the garden, she came to the largest of the fountains and paused, glancing up to her own windows where the lights she had left burning were partially obscured by the spreading leaves of the flame tree.

What name should she decide on for her hero? she wondered, frowning. Oddly enough, she had toyed with 'Ramón' before coming to Mexico, but it had too familiar a ring to satisfy her. 'Román' would have given her character the distinction she sought, she reflected regretfully, but knowing its true owner she couldn't possibly. . .

'Are you flesh and blood, or a figment of my fanciful imagination?' said Román from behind, his voice amusedly soft.

Laura whirled on a choked gasp, her hand going instinctively to the low front of her negligee. He looked like an apparition himself in luminous white shirt and the same black trousers he had worn for dinner.

Her voice sounding strangled in her throat, she demanded, 'What are you doing here?' with ludicrous disregard for the fact that the house and grounds were his to stroll in as he pleased.

'Presumably like yourself, *señorita*, sleep evaded me.' He stepped closer until she could see the faint glitter of moonlight in his black eyes. The rich odour of cigar smoke drifted to her nostrils at the same time as she saw the thin cylinder with its ashy red tip in his right hand.

'I—I didn't know you smoked,' she said stupidly, reaching desperately for some way of diverting his lazy attention from the line of her throat where it emerged from the soft blue of her wrap, inwardly cursing her thoughtlessness at wandering the property at this late hour in her nightclothes. She saw him shrug.

'I don't very much. Tonight I succumbed to weakness.' At last his eyes lifted to stare mockingly into hers. 'And you? What brings you to wander the moonlit garden like a beautiful nymph?'

The flowery phrases, flattering though no doubt insincere coming from him, brought an icy stiffness into Laura's, 'Only an inability to sleep, *señor*. I'm sorry if I disturbed you, please excuse me.' When she sidestepped around him, he turned with her and his left hand fastened firmly on her forearm.

'It is not necessary for you to leave, Laura,' he said, a strange quality coming into his voice, almost as if—but Román Castillo pleaded with no woman, she told herself tautly. His fingers burned searingly through the flimsy sleeves of her robe, and she jerked her arm away as if she had indeed been burned. 'This might be a good opportunity to become better acquainted, you and I.'

'I'm not exactly dressed for socialising, Señor Castillo,' she retorted drily, her fingers aching with the tightness of her grip on her robe. 'Besides, I—need quiet moments like this to think about my work.'

'Ah, your work' he nodded thoughtfully. 'It was my impression that you were thinking pensively of your lover when I came upon you.'

'My—what?' she asked, startled.

'Was that not what my aunt referred to when she spoke of your past troubles?' He looked at the cigar in his hand, then tossed it aside. 'Come, *chica*, sit down here and tell me about it.'

Darn Isabel! fumed Laura as he took her arm again to lead her to a white padded wrought iron sofa situated beneath the flame tree's spreading branches. Darn herself for sparking the older woman's curiosity by raking up a love affair long dead. She found herself seated beside the casually relaxed Román on the confined space of the sofa and felt uncomfortable with the situation, but to fly out of his presence would simply make her look foolish and as if she had something to hide.

'There's nothing to tell, *señor*,' she said flatly, her spine held rigid against the patterned back of the settee because Román's arm was draped negligently across it and she could have sworn she felt the heat of his flesh radiating to hers. 'Your aunt imagined, when I confided in her, that I'm still bothered by something that happened years ago.'

'And you are not?'

'Certainly not. My work absorbs me too much to leave time for useless moping about what might have been.'

'Yet you are very beautiful,' his hand lifted to the gold sheen of her hair and played distractedly with one bright strand, running it like silk through his fingers. 'Surely it is not natural for such a beautiful woman to be without a lover who appreciates her.'

A small battle, silent but potent, developed between them as Laura sought to free her head and he clung determinedly on to the hair, hurting her scalp as the roots tugged between his unyielding fingers.

'I came here to work, *señor*,' she stressed the title, 'not to find romance. Like you, I'm content to play the field for a while longer,' she ended boldly, turning the level blue of her eyes on him and gratified to feel his grip relax on her hair. 'I'm sure your love life is a lot more interesting than mine, anyway,' she spoke again when he remained silent. 'Are you going to marry Mercedes?'

He gave a visible start. 'Mercedes? What gave you that idea?'

'She's beautiful,' Laura shrugged, able to leave but strangely reluctant to do so now, 'and she has the kind of background that would suit a man like you—good family, social graces, and—she loves you.'

The dark brows winged upward in surprise. 'What makes you think that? Whatever your reasons, I assure you they are wrong,' he tacked on hastily, seeming almost embarrassed by the spotlight on his own romantic life.

Laura suddenly felt she had the upper hand. 'I don't think so. I *do* think that you're being impossibly old-fashioned to expect her to give up her career for marriage.'

'Am I that?' he asked, seeming as startled as she herself had been moments before.

'Old-fashioned? Yes, of course you are if you expect the woman you marry to give up a very important part of her life.'

'You would not want to do that?' he asked, seeming absorbed in the hypothetical question, 'to become a wife and mother?'

'They're not mutually exclusive, you know! Millions of women today have work outside the home, and their husbands and children are better for it.'

'But you would want children, although your work is so very important to you?' he pursued with almost academic interest, which relaxed Laura into warm helpfulness in Mercedes' cause—she had liked the Mexican woman very much, and knew that to cut her off from her unique talents would be nothing less than a sin.

'Of course I would,' she said emphatically. 'Some women choose not to have a family, and that's fine—coming from a small family myself, I'd like to have a houseful!'

'That could pose problems,' he retorted with what she felt was a rare flash of wry humour, 'if your husband offered a very large house with many bedrooms.'

'True,' she laughed, genuinely liking him for the first time and feeling a twinge of envy for the lovely Mercedes who held his heart in her small palms. Her fertile imagination leapt ahead to the chuckles of black-haired children tumbling through the mansion with noisy exuberance. Lucky Mercedes, she sighed.

'Come,' Román rose and held out one olive-skinned hand for her to clasp. As she glided to her feet, a wistful darkening in her eyes, he pulled her close to the firm outline of his body and let his gaze linger on the planes and hollows of her face as the moon's light touched them.

'You have lost enough sleep for one night. Tomorrow, what was troubling you tonight will seem much clearer, I promise you.'

Strangely, she believed him. For a moment she thought he was about to kiss her, his deepset eyes were so intent as if memorising every contour of her face, but then he slid one hand down her arm and clasped her hand to lead her to the soft lights of the patio. In the hall he went as far as the staircase with her and then brushed his lips across the hand still warm from his touch.

'*Buenas noches*, Laura,' he murmured, seeming suddenly formal as he stood back and watched her retreat up the elegant staircase.

Her feet seemed strangely light, as if they barely touched the thick red carpet slashed across the white marble stairs or the upper hall that led to her room. Once inside, she went quickly to the window above the desk and saw the lights opposite snap on. Román's shadow moved behind the half-transparent blinds of his living room before that was plunged into darkness and the bedroom lights, immediately opposite her own, flashed on. Then, feeling like a Peeping Tom, she moved from the window and switched off her own lights, sliding out of the negligee and into bed in almost one smooth motion.

Hands clasped behind her head as she stared at the dark ceiling, she found sleep continued to elude her. But now her thoughts were entirely different from the ones that had plagued her earlier.

Entirely different. . .

CHAPTER FOUR

IN spite of her sleepless night, Laura was up, dressed and working at her desk when Rosa brought her breakfast tray in the morning. The shy young maid looked nonplussed, not knowing where to place the tray, and Laura, smiling, patted the desk top beside her papers.

'It's such a lovely morning I decided to make an early start on my work,' she explained in the Spanish that was becoming so fluent that she was scarcely aware of whether she conversed in that or English.

'*Si, señorita.*' Rosa put down the tray and cast a puzzled look at the handwritten notes Laura was making. 'You are studying, *señorita?*'

Laura laughed wryly. 'No, but sometimes I wish I were! It's a lot easier to learn things that other people have written than to write them yourself.'

The soft brown eyes widened in amazement. 'You are a—a *professor?*'

'Heavens, no! I'm a writer of fiction.'

'Ah.' Respect mingled with the wonder. 'You must be very clever, *señorita.*'

'Not really, I'm just doing something I like to do.' That truism hadn't existed for her until she woke this morning and found herself alive with new slants on her characters, particularly Felipe Alvarez—she had even woken with her hero's name on her lips.

'Oh, I forget,' Rosa drew her eyes from the

67

handwriting that was incomprehensible to her.
'Señora Castillo wishes to know if you will be
shopping with her this morning as planned.'

A frown sliced between Laura's brows. Isabel
was nothing if not persistent! She had no more
desire to go shopping for clothes, which she hated
to do at the best of times, than to fly back
unaided to New York. At this moment, she felt as
if she could work on for ever, her thoughts
coming thick and fast. Yet—she supposed she *did*
owe Isabel a debt of gratitude for making this
visit possible, and the older woman was obviously
hungry for female company in doing what
obviously absorbed most of her interest.

'Tell the Señora I'll be happy to join her,' she
sighed, 'whenever she's ready.'

Irritated to find that the mood for work had
vanished, she poured coffee and leaned back in
the desk chair, staring out to the balcony where
the sun struck through the flame tree in shafts to
the tiled floor. On an impulse, she opened the
doors and carried her tray out to the round table,
shifting it to the edge of the balcony and dragging
a chair after it. From that vantage point, she
could enjoy the neatly laid out and colourful
gardens below. The central fountain, its tiered
cups of old stone making it look as if it had been
there for ever, had been turned on and the sun
transformed each droplet of water into a
miniature kaleidoscope of vivid colours.

For the first time, Laura felt a pang of regret at
leaving the beautiful old place when her work was
done. It was like something from another age, as
if time had stood still amidst the maelstrom of the
modern world outside the stout walls. The

gardener who bent over a triangular flower bed in the far corner, his wide-brimmed straw hat shielding face and neck from the fierce sun, had a timelessness about him that spoke of countless generations before him doing exactly the same thing in the same way.

Her mouth parted in a small smile. At least Román couldn't be accused of having stood still in line with his ancestors, at least not in all ways. He was a product of both worlds, old and new, with his reverence for long-held traditions liberally sprinkled with the hard-nosed business qualities expected of a man in his position today. What would Don Román, his lookalike ancestor, have thought of his namesake's aggressive business practices? Apparently he himself devoted his attention to constraining his flighty wife; she could never imagine Román doing that, she mused solemnly. But then, no wife of his would want to look at another man. . .

His mocking voice floated up to the balcony. 'You look pensive enough to be thinking of a lost lover, *señorita*, but I am learning something about you, so my guess is that you are deeply involved in planning your new book. Am I right?'

Laura looked dazedly down, still lost in thoughts that had nothing to do with her book, and saw a Román who radiated health and vitality and supreme disregard for the heat of the sun on his well-cut dark suit. His hair glinted blue-black and seemed still damp from the shower.

'I—yes, I guess I was,' she admitted uncomfortably, hating to lie, but she could hardly tell him that she had been daydreaming about him and the wife he would have one day. Seeing him standing looking up at her, a briefcase in his hand and an open, friendly smile on his face, she felt a surge of warm colour to her face and body.

'Too much work is not good for you, Laura. As you are my guest, I think I must do something about that.' He looked so fierce for a moment that Laura wondered hysterically if he possessed, after all, the sadistic tendencies of his ancestor.

'Your aunt obviously has the same idea,' she laughed nervously. 'I'm going shopping with her later this morning.'

'Good. Then you can both have lunch with me—tell my aunt to bring you to my offices at one sharp. Now, as I have an appointment at ten, please excuse me. *Hasta la vista*, Laura.'

With a quick bend of his arm he strode away in the direction of the garages at the rear, and Laura let out a sigh she hadn't been aware of holding. Isabel would no doubt be thrilled that her strategy was seemingly working, but Laura wasn't at all sure she wanted to visit the lion in his business den. She much preferred him the way he had been last night in the moonlit garden, his hard edges blurred, which made him more human and approachable. So much so that on waking this morning she had decided that her treatment of her hero was much too rigid, one-sided. No one was all black or all white, a rounded character had elements of both.

However, she selected a sweet roll and buttered it absently; visiting Román in his offices would be invaluable as background material for the book, since her hero moved in the fast-paced world of business.

*　　*　　*

Shopping with Isabel had a nightmarish quality that exhausted Laura before they entered their third exclusive salon. Everything in the store had to be brought out for their inspection, and Isabel made impulsive, and shockingly expensive, decisions for Laura as well as herself. The news that Román had invited them for lunch seemingly inspired the greatest frenzy of buying.

'You see, I was right,' Isabel crowed with satisfaction. 'I knew he could never resist your golden hair and fair skin ... your colouring is very attractive to our men, you know,' she prattled on, distractedly appraising a multi-hued creation that would suit neither of them. 'Do you think this one——?'

'No,' Laura said emphatically, turning the older woman's attention to a draped style in old rose that would be becoming of her age and figure. 'Why don't you try this?'

Isabel's nose wrinkled distastefully. 'Such a dull colour, I really prefer——'

'It would hurt nothing to try it on, *señora*,' the elegant saleslady backed Laura up. 'Meanwhile, I can show the *señorita* a very special new creation. . .' She led the mollified Isabel away, and Laura turned with little interest to the wide-spaced dresses on a nearby rod. Some of the colours attracted her, but the styles were too faddish for her. She liked simplicity with a first-class cut, and nothing on the rack appealed to her.

The saleswoman came, flustered, from the carpeted dressing rooms and gave her a taut smile. 'Ah, yes, *señorita*, let me show you the dress I mentioned.'

'I'm really not looking,' Laura began, letting her voice peter out when the woman hurried away to the rear of the salon. Shrugging, she turned and stared in amazement at the transformed Isabel who emerged from the dressing room frowning.

'You see what I mean? There is no colour in this dress at all!'

'Oh, *señora*, it's perfect for you!'

The dress was truly stunning, its soft colour flattering Isabel's fading skin and giving it life, the cleverly draped folds minimising her figure faults and emphasising the good points.

'You think so?' the older woman doubted, looking down at herself then up when the saleswoman came back bearing a shimmering gold dress across her arms. Irritably, she said, 'That's no good for me, I can see from here that it's too small.'

'It was for the young lady to try,' the woman retorted drily, holding the dress by its hanger to let Laura see its simple perfection.

'Oh . . . well, yes, I can see it might fit you, Laura. Why don't you try it?'

Tempted as Laura was, she declined. 'Where would I wear a dress like that?' she objected. 'And it probably cost more than I spend in a year on clothes.'

Isabel's head lifted proudly. 'A lady does not consider the cost when it comes to being well dressed. As for where you will wear it, there will be many occasions when Román will want you at his side, and you cannot dishonour him by appearing in something inferior.'

Exasperated, Laura's mouth tightened stubbornly. 'I only buy what I can afford, *señora*, and this is way beyond my means.'

'It will be taken care of,' Isabel insisted haughtily. 'Help the *señorita* try it on,' she commanded the watchful saleswoman, who sprang into action and swept Laura off to the dressing room before she had time to make further objections. Skilled as she was, she had recognised the longing look in Laura's deep blue eyes when they lit on the dress.

Unfortunately for Laura's stand, the dress fitted her slender curves perfectly, and even her reluctant viewing could not deny the gown's rightness for her. The shimmering folds falling to below the knee picked up the same rich highlights in her hair and made them sparkle too. The cunningly cut bodice might have been specially made to contour her breasts to a tasteful yet provocative neckline.

'But I'd never wear it,' she said weakly, turning this way and that in front of the triple mirrors.

'Just once, *señorita*,' the saleswoman promised seductively, 'and the man of your dreams will be yours.'

The man of her dreams? There wasn't such a one, unless it was Felipe Alvarez, the arrogant hero of her novel. But Laura let the enthusiastic woman draw her out to the foyer where Isabel waited impatiently, though her frown lifted immediately when she saw Laura.

'*Dios*,' she breathed, 'you are *magnifica* in that dress, and it fits you as if made for you. She will take it,' she ordered, turning to the almost purring saleswoman. 'And I will take this,

although I still have doubts about it. Charge
them to my account.'

'No, *señora*,' Laura protested firmly, 'I'll pay
for it myself, or I won't accept it.' Why not?
Heaven alone knew where she would wear it, but
after the success of her first book she could afford
to splash a little, just once. It took time to re-
budget for greater affluence, especially when a
frivolous dress like this was concerned.

Her guilt about buying it lasted until she and
Isabel were ushered into Román's starkly modern
office, sparsely but tastefully furnished in teak
with colour provided by the abstract paintings
placed strategically here and there. The secretary
who led them into the office smiled tightly at
Isabel and stared insolently at Laura, her dark
eyes seeming to flash contempt for her reddish-
fair colouring, which was emphasised by the
green and blue hues of her simply cut sleeveless
dress. A superior smile etched her full-carved
mouth when she announced them to Román, who
sat in shirt sleeves behind a massive desk in the
far corner of the room where light from the floor-
length windows to his right fell on the jumble of
papers and folders strewn across the desk.

She's in love with him, Laura thought
dispassionately, as which secretary wouldn't be if
her boss was single, good-looking, and wealthy to
boot? It amused her a little to think that the dark
girl was concerned at her presence—hadn't she
heard of Mercedes?

Román reached for the jacket hitched across
the back of his chair and shrugged it on as he
came round the desk to greet them, smoothing
the thick dark lines of his hair which looked as if

he had run distracted hands through it more than
once. Laura preferred his dishevelled look, it
made him more human somehow.

'Tia Isabel—Laura,' he took a hand of each
and smiled in welcome, though Laura sensed a
distraction far down in his black eyes. 'I had no
idea it was so late, I've been so busy this
morning. May I offer you a drink before we go to
lunch?' Dropping Isabel's hand but retaining
Laura's to draw her over to a seating area of sofa
and sparsely outlined but comfortable chairs, he
enquired what they would like.

'I know you will have Scotch and soda, Tia
Isabel,' he smiled, turning to Laura, 'but I am
not yet acquainted with your tastes, Laura.'

She would have preferred a large cup of
bracing coffee after the morning's shopping, but
that might cause problems with the secretary who
would perhaps have to bring it from elsewhere, so
she asked for a medium sherry if he had it.

'I have a little of everything here,' he said
drily, crossing to a concealed liquor cabinet that
opened at the touch of his finger to display an
array of beverages to satisfy the most demanding
tastes. He prepared the drinks on the shelf
immediately under the bottle display, taking a
light beer from the built in bar refrigerator and
pouring it into a glass for himself. A slight
stiffness in his movements made Laura wonder if
they had perhaps interrupted important business.
In an office like this, business obviously took top
priority.

'If it's not convenient for us to be here,' she
began as he handed a cut crystal sherry glass to
her, 'we can——'

'Of course not,' his forceful denial over-whelmed Isabel's disappointed exclamation. 'I have the rest of the day to tie up loose ends. So— *salud!*' Lifting his glass in toast, he looked round irritably when a tap sounded on the door and his secretary came in, bristling with importance.

'What is it, Martha?' If Laura had been his secretary and he had spoken to her in that manner, she would have either shrivelled up or sparked back at him. The sultry Martha did neither.

'Señor Garcia is on the telephone, and he says he must see you today about the contract,' she said with flat nonchalance.

'*Dios!* Tell him to talk with my cousin, who has been negotiating the contract.'

Martha shrugged. 'He says he must speak with you or no one, that Señor Nicolas is never available.'

'He is available now,' Román retorted sharply. 'I spoke to him not long ago in the office.'

'He left for lunch just after you spoke with him,' she said smugly, 'and left no telephone number where he could be reached.'

Román cursed again and got to his feet. 'Put Señor Garcia through to me,' he ordered grimly, apologising to his guests before striding over to his desk and picking up one of the vari-coloured phones lined up to one side of it.

'Does he expect the boy to work all day with nothing in his stomach?' Isabel complained in a strident whisper to Laura, her eyes snapping as they concentrated on Román's tensely set face.

After the preliminary of courteous greeting, his voice took on an edged politeness. '*Si, señor*, I understand your problem, but the contract was negotiated by my cousin and you must conduct all further business with him.' He listened for a moment, then went on with deadly calm, 'I see. Yes, you are right to speak to me, I knew nothing of these terms my cousin insists on ... yes, certainly we have conducted business many times in the past, and with fair conditions. Leave me to deal with it, Ricardo. *Adios*.'

White temper lines etched the skin at either side of his forceful mouth when he slammed down the telephone and gave Isabel a scathing look that made her draw herself up defensively.

'Not only does your son spend less time in his office than anyone else I have ever known, but he has succeeded in offending a long-standing business associate of mine. As I have told you many times, *tia*, he is totally unsuited to this kind of work, which needs dedication and loyalty and a sense of responsibility. He possesses none of these qualities.'

He had remained at his desk, but now he rose impatiently, his long, lean figure taut with barely repressed anger as he came back to join them.

'But what could he do if you throw him out, Román?' Isabel cried shrilly. 'He is young still,' she switched to cajolery, 'and he has time to learn, if only you will be less harsh with him. Can you not talk to him as a father would, explain——'

'I am not his father,' Román interrupted in weary repetition of what Nicolas had loudly stated on Laura's arrival at the Villa Castillo, 'and I have no wish to assume paternity for an indolent young man like Nicolas, who has failed to take advantage of every opportunity I have given him.' He glanced at Laura as if suddenly remembering her presence. 'I hope you will forgive our ill manners, Laura, in conducting a family argument in your presence, and I promise there will be no more of it during lunch, which' he glanced at his slim gold watch, 'we should be heading towards at this moment if you have finished your drink.'

Laura hastily set her half-finished drink on the low teak table and stood. 'Yes, of course.' Reaching for her handbag, she tried to inject a note of lightness into the atmosphere. 'I must confess to being starved after our morning's shopping, so I hope I won't break your lunch budget.'

'I think the budget will not be strained,' he said, evidently restored to humour, 'although the seams of your very delightful dress may be if you are as ravenous as you say. Are you ready, Tia Isabel?'

The older woman swallowed the last of her drink swiftly and struggled to her feet. 'I am ready, Román,' she said with cool dignity, 'but perhaps you feel I should stay and talk to Nicolas when he returns.'

Román frowned impatiently. 'You have more than enough time for lunch, and probably dinner too, before that happens. And your talks with him in the past have not been very effective, have they? I think that what that young man needs is a cold shock to his system to force him into recognising his responsibilities, but then,' he threw up his hands, then used them to pilot the two women from the room, 'I promised there would be no more of this, at least until we have eaten.' The secretary gave them a sulky look from behind her typewriter, and he said pleasantly, 'You can go to lunch now, Martha, I won't be returning until four.'

Laura was startled until she recalled the leisurely fashion of Mexican meals, where waiters felt they would be insulting their clients by hurrying them in any respect. She wasn't at all sure that that tranquilly drawn out lunch hour wouldn't be welcome today. Her feet ached from walking around stores and standing interminably while clothes were tried and either bought or rejected. It would be nice to relax and have nothing whatever to think about except what she would choose from the menu.

And an extensive menu it was in the private club Román escorted them to, being received obsequiously by the *maitre d'* and ushered to a table laid for three by the window, which overlooked a quiet, shaded patio garden. There were tables out there too, and Laura wished for a moment that Román had decided on that location, but after reflection knew that it was far too informal for his rather stiff personality. She could never imagine him relaxing to the extent that the sprinkling of tourists did out there in their bright coloured holiday wear.

'Will you allow me to choose a pre-lunch drink for you?' he asked as soon as they were settled, not waiting for her answer as he spoke quickly and unintelligibly to the waiter.

'I hope it's nothing too strong, I'm not much of a drinker,' she protested as the waiter moved away, 'especially in the middle of the afternoon.'

'You will have only one,' he decreed auto-cratically, 'and you will be surprised at how much you will enjoy the meal to follow. Will you also allow me to choose that?'

If an escort in the States had asked her such a question, she would have indignantly refused, but she was out of her depth here and would probably make an idiot of herself by choosing entirely unsuitable dishes. Her eyes were cool, though, as they met the amused glint of question in his.

'Thank you, but nothing very hot, please.'

'It is not necessary for our dishes to be burning to the tongue, *señorita*. Is that not so, *tia*?' he turned to Isabel on his left, drawing her attention from the adjoining tables occupied by several people known to her.

'What did you say, Román?' she asked in an abstracted murmur. He repeated his question, and she nodded vigorously. 'Of course, you may have them as picant as you wish. I remember your mother telling me,' she smiled at Laura reminiscently, 'how you hated the fiery dishes and refused to eat them, although she and your father enjoyed them.'

'They got used to spicy dishes in India before I was born,' she retorted drily. 'Unfortunately, I didn't inherit their cast-iron tongues!'

'You must have led an interesting life with your family,' Román remarked, signalling when the drinks waiter returned to indicate placement of the glasses. Laura's was a wide shallow one encrusted with salt around the rim as well as a thick wedge of fresh lime, crushed ice blending with the colourless liquor in the glass. 'To live in so many different places is an excellent education.'

'You must read her book,' interjected Isabel after taking a hasty sip of her inevitable whisky and soda. 'It's about the daughter of a diplomat and the exciting life she has, meeting important people and falling in love with half of them, is that not so?' she smiled archly at Laura. 'Quite true to life, I would think.'

Colour rose and diffused itself over Laura's neck and face, vulnerably open because of the neat severity of her hairstyle, drawn back from the high cheekbones and fastened in a loose chignon at her nape.

'The backgrounds are drawn from places I visited,' she said tightly, 'but the emotional stuff is strictly imagination.'

'Oh, come now,' Isabel chided slyly, 'wasn't the English diplomat modelled on the one who made you so unhappy? He was married, too, and had children—oh!' Too late, she recalled her pledge of silence.

'It all sounds fascinating,' Román drawled uninterestedly, glancing at the menu opened before him. 'Why don't you try your drink, Laura, and tell me what you think of it?'

Appreciating his lack of curiosity into what Isabel had made sound like a lurid past, Laura took a larger gulp than she had intended—and stared frozen-eyed at Román as a fiery liquid coursed down her throat and left her breath trapped somewhere below it. Heat exploded in her taste buds despite the crushed ice she had swallowed too, and she stared at him in gasping dismay, hating the smile of amusement that touched his sensually formed mouth.

'Take another sip,' he commanded, 'only not such a large one, perhaps.'

Striving for nonchalance, she did so, and found the repeat a pale replica of the first gulp. In fact, not unpleasant at all. 'What is it?' she voiced hoarsely.

'A drink based on our national plant, the *maguey*,' he explained coolly.

'Tequila?'

'*Si*. With a few additions that turn it into a *margarita* cocktail, at which the barman here excels.'

'I'm afraid he won't be mixing any more for me today,' Laura said tartly, and saw Román shake his head.

'As I have said, one is plenty, two would be far too much for someone unused to it. Now, with your permission, I will plan the meal.'

He did just that, frowning over the thick leather-framed menu, and later Laura knew that she could never have selected so finely herself. A pickled fish dish, *seviche*, was followed by clear soup delightfully flavoured, then braised veal in cream sauce accompanied by crisp cooked vegetables, and to end with a caramel-flavoured custard that nicely coated the palate. With the meal, Román selected a light Mexican wine that blended innocuously with the food.

'I congratulate you, *señor*,' Laura complimented gravely, only pleasantly glowing from the combined drinks, as he had promised. 'I can't remember enjoying another meal more.'

He shrugged, but she could tell he was pleased. 'It will be my pleasure to introduce you to other restaurants in Guadalajara while you are here. Do you like French food?'

She nodded. 'Love it, but I can find that anywhere. I'd really like to try as much as possible of the Mexican offerings before I leave.' A wistful cast came down over her eyes ... there was suddenly something bleakly forlorn about the thought of leaving this country that exuded the joy of life in every street corner, every lined peasant's face, every lovingly tended garden.

'Then I will take you to a very special place at our artisans' centre in Tlaquepaque,' he announced. 'A place so special that no name could be found for it, so it is known as just that—the Restaurant No-Name.'

'Really?' she grinned delightedly.

'Really,' he returned gravely. 'In fact I will take you there this coming Saturday. We will spend the afternoon seeing what the artisans have to offer, and then we will dine at the Restaurant No-Name.'

'But won't——?' began Laura, about to ask if Mercedes wouldn't mind, when Isabel withdrew from the moody clouds that had swirled around her all through lunch.

'An excellent suggestion, Román, though I will not be able to accompany you on that day. I must attend the fair organised by the church's charity committee, but I am sure that it is quite ethical for you to dine alone together.'

'My dear *tia*,' Román retorted drily, his olive features more reminiscent of his ancestor Don Román than a product of the twentieth century, 'I believe I can be trusted to entertain a guest in my house without incurring the censure of your moralistic friends.'

'Yes, of course, *caro*,' she agreed, her expression lightening several degrees, 'of course.'

Laura stopped looking mesmerically from one to the other of them, her attention drawn inwardly to the warm glow of excitement stirring deep within her. More than anything else in the world, she wanted to go with him wherever he dictated, wanted to prolong and deepen the intimacy that had flashed between them since the time she had walked into his office . . . perhaps even before that.

CHAPTER FIVE

On Saturday, Isabel waved them off as Román eased the chocolate brown Chrysler through the narrow back gateway into the busy street. Already her mind was on the commitee meeting to come, and she had obviously forgotten her qualms about the unchaperoned visit of her nephew and guest to the artisans' centre.

Laura wasn't nearly so unconcerned as the luxury car glided to a halt and purred powerfully while awaiting the change of traffic signal. It wasn't so much the plush beige bucket seat that wrapped comfort around her thighs, but the devastatingly handsome man who sat beside her that set up the taut constriction in her throat. The casual sports shirt that left the top half of his chest exposed in a flurry of dark, twisted hairs, the beige trousers that emphasised the lean tautness of his thighs and stomach—those were the things that made her feel gauche, out of her depth in a way she hadn't experienced for years.

Glad that Román was absorbed in his driving, she glanced out and saw that they were on Avenue Vallarta, a main thoroughfare that had seen extensive renovations in recent years, street widening and the erection of smart office blocks and commercial enterprises. Only a few of the magnificent old Spanish-Moorish mansions such as the Villa Castillo had been spared the wreckers' havoc. It was a pity, she thought idly, occupying herself with trying to visualise what it must have been like before the age of cars, when fancy carriages rumbled over the cobbled streets . . . probably a lot noisier than it was now, despite the vastly increased traffic.

'Something is troubling you?' Román asked quietly, meeting her startled gaze for a moment before turning his attention back to the milling trucks, buses and cars.

'No, of course not,' she denied lightly. 'I was just wondering what it must have been like here a hundred years ago, before all this.' She gestured to the scene around them just as a passing bus emitted clouds of noxious diesel fumes, and Román winced.

'Certainly it was healthier for the lungs in those days,' he made the dry comment, then turned to glance at her again. 'If you would really like to know about the old Guadalajara, I have some old prints of the city as it used to be in different eras, as well as some ancient manuscripts that describe the day-to-day lives of the inhabitants. But perhaps you do not need such detail for your book?'

'Oh no!—yes!—I mean,' she coloured furiously at her own ineptitude, 'the book is set in today's world, but there are—undertones from the past, so the more I know the better equipped I'll be to write it.'

'Aha, undertones of the past,' he teased, steering between a ferociously panting giant truck and a tiny Volkswagen. 'I learn a little more each time I am with you about this new saga of yours. Am I permitted to guess just a little as to its contents?—or are you truly a reclusive writer?'

'No, I—well, I don't know what I am yet, I have very little experience.'

'M-mm,' he agreed, putting a world of meaning into the simple utterance, telling Laura that he wasn't thinking entirely of literary experience. 'Well,' he mused, 'I would guess that your *novella* is concerned with the eternal triangle, no? And that the man is one of substance, of aristocratic background, which causes problems in his present-day relationships. No, don't tell me I am wrong yet!' he took a hand off the steering wheel to ward off her incredulous exclamation. 'I am enjoying this, and it helps me not to get too angry at other drivers who are, of course, much more reckless, more stupid than I!'

Glancing at him, Laura realised that he was indeed relaxing in a way that would appeal to his intellectual, if imperious, nature, as another man would have delighted in solving a difficult crossword puzzle. How much he was relaxing was proved in his poking fun at his own foibles.

'So . . . we have this man, and presumably two opposing love interests . . . two women, one he is perhaps obligated to by ties of responsibility—a wife? Yes. But there is also this other member of the triangle . . . the one who is important for other reasons. Does she supply the qualities his wife lacks? Youth, beauty? *Dios!* ' he cursed, swerving to avoid the car in front which had made an unexpected turn into a side street. 'So where were we?' he resumed as if nothing had intervened, slanting a sideways look at Laura and immediately tightening his hands on the wheel. 'What is it, Laura, is something wrong?'

She had felt the colour draining from her

cheeks as his accurate speculations continued, and her eyes felt enormous as she exchanged his glance. 'It's you who should be the writer, *señor*,' she said in a small, tight voice, 'not me.'

'Ah—forgive me, I had no idea that my stupid chatter would have meaning for you.' He did indeed look desperately penitent, so much so that Laura injected a note of shaky humour.

'Do you mind if I borrow some of your ideas? I'd pay you collaborator's fees.'

He threw back his head and laughed, more freely than she would ever have imagined possible. 'I would earn very little, *pequeña*! I am a man of ideas, but never ask me to clothe them in words. It would be impossible for me. That is why,' he threw her a melting glance of admiration, 'creative people like you must be cherished. And I will begin as of this moment.'

Laura had scarcely noticed the narrow one-way streets they had travelled to reach the parking lot at the village centre ... now she saw with surprise that they were wedged between a station wagon and a small passenger car on the second level of the garage. Román took her hand as she wiggled through the narrow space, and retained his hold as he led her down the cement steps to the next level, which was redolent with the aromas of the fresh food market which was now winding down for the day. Through a long covered alley into the crowded, narrow street, and Laura was so fascinated by the bustle of life around her that she neglected to withdraw her hand from his, tightening her hold instead whenever anything particularly caught her eye.

'Oh, look, Román, those gorgeous Nativity

scenes, so beautifully carved,' she drew him over to a narrow shop window and gazed enraptured at the cleverly executed carvings.

'We are drawing close to the Christmas season,' he remarked drily, 'so you will no doubt see many of these.'

'Oh, you're such a cut-and-dried commercialist!' she reproved, but she was glad that she could uninhibitedly admire whatever caught her fancy without feeling, as with most men, that he would feel obliged to buy it for her. Particularly since her enthusiasm ran from red clay garden pots all the way to the exquisitely coloured semi-precious stones in intricate settings.

They watched for a while the artist who painted freestyle with a palette knife, and a carver who wrought exceedingly delicate creations out of glistening white softstone, wandering from there to the patio gardens where they were entertained by *mariachi* players as they sipped on *margaritas* at a table close to a celebration party.

'It's been a lovely day,' Laura looked happily across the table at a Román who seemed to have loosed the onerous ties of business for this one afternoon. His ascetically contoured face was easier to read, somehow, without the overlay of his businessman image. His deepset eyes, burning like dark coals, were amusedly relaxed as he watched her reactions. His white smile flashed frequently, highlighting his prominent cheekbones and drawing her attention to the sensuous fullness of his lips. The strong dark brows were raised far more often than they were lowered in a frown, making it easy to imagine his vulnerability as a young man before the weight of responsibility had descended upon him.

'You speak as if the day is already over,' he commented with a smile, 'but there is still the evening, when we will have dinner together.'

A shiver of anticipation ran through Laura, though the thought of Mercedes toned it down somewhat. It was unethical to feel this thrilled over the prospect of spending an evening in the company of another woman's man. Still, if Mercedes really cared about him, would she have turned him loose on the all-important Saturday night?

'You seem deep in thought,' Román said softly. 'May I be permitted to ask what demons bring that frown to your usually smooth brow?'

The flowery phrasing at another time might have amused her, but now it brought a deepening of the grooves between her brows. 'I was wondering about Mercedes,' she said in a clipped voice. 'Shouldn't you be spending the evening with her?'

'Mercedes?' He seemed genuinely puzzled, but for a man who could so rapidly concoct a plot for a three-cornered situation, it was naïve in the extreme. 'Why should you think that what Mercedes does with her evenings in Guadalajara is of any concern to me?'

Laura blinked, her fingers tightening round the shallow bowl of her glass. 'Well, aren't you——? I mean, I gathered that you and Mercedes were——'

'Lovers?' he supplied coolly. 'That may be Tia Isabel's conviction, but I assure you it has no relevance to the truth. Mercedes and I have been close since childhood,' he went on to explain, 'and because of that we are very good friends. As for anything else,' he shrugged, 'we are simply good friends.'

'But——' Laura stopped abruptly, uncertain of her ground. If Mercedes meant nothing to him in a romantic sense, that left the field clear for— Lord, not for her, he probably had women oozing from his well-formed ears!

'But?' he repeated quizzically, black brows arching over the amused glitter in his deepset eyes.

Laura made a gesture with her hand. 'There must be someone special in your life—after all, you're not——' she was about to say 'young' and corrected herself hastily, 'a callow youth. Isn't it important for you to settle down and provide heirs to your—house?'

'Very important,' he agreed gravely, though there was still a gleam of humour deep in his eyes. 'Until now, no eligible female has appealed to me as a permanent fixture in my life.'

Until now? What did that mean? Was there someone else, a woman she, or more particularly Tia Isabel, was not aware of? And what business of hers was it, after all, she thought drily, blinking as Román reached across the table and turned her palm upward to his inquisitive gaze.

'And what of you, *cariña*? If I were a palmist I could perhaps see your past and future in these delightful lines and curves in your hand, but since I am not I must rely on you to enlighten me. Is there a lover in your life?'

A rose flush darkened her cheeks in unison with her quick denial. 'Of course not. Men are a little scared of women who are successful in their own right,' she added with a touch of bitterness, recalling the awed admiration of several young men on the fringes of literary circles who had remained in the 'awed' category.

Román shrugged, his finger tracing outlines absentmindedly, and disturbingly, on the sensitive surface of her palm. 'That is understandable, perhaps. Men still have this—primitive desire to be greater in a worldly sense than the woman he gives his heart to. His instinct is to shield, protect, the most vulnerable part of him, which is his love for a woman. This is perhaps why your married lover was torn between remaining with his wife or exposing you to the raised eyebrows of diplomatic circles.'

The change of subject was so sudden that Laura gasped, her eyes darkening as she took in the gist of what he was saying. Finally, she managed to utter a faint, 'Your aunt was so anxious to hear details of my romantic life that I—I told her about Gavin. But that was over long ago.'

His eyes seemed to pierce hers and reach down into her soul.

'Good,' he said slowly, finally, gathering himself together with obvious effort. 'Now, what would you like to see?'

They wandered again, this time with a somehow freer hip-to-hip pace, a more open touching of their hands in clasping together. Laura felt numb, as if her senses were held in abeyance for this afternoon, thoughts of the past and future blocked out. She bought a pair of pottery ducks for Eleanor, her mother, knowing she would enjoy the pert humour in their expressions. A small iron replica of a Colonial soldier braced for action would serve for her father. Her brother was more difficult to shop for, but finally she found a woven hanging which depicted a blunt-nosed eagle with wings spread to indicate strength. Mike would like that.

'If you have no more shopping to do,' Román said finally, glancing at his watch, 'we should make our way to the restaurant.'

'The one that doesn't have a name?' she teased, conscious of a happy shine on her nose as she glanced up at him. That would be remedied, she told herself, as soon as they reached the legendary restaurant. 'Lead on, *señor*!'

'*Si*,' he concurred gravely, then smiled and sent her heart into an uneven rhythm that left her breathless. Tucking her arm into his for support, he stepped with shortened strides that suited her towards the unheralded, unnamed restaurant.

In the entrance patio let into the wall from the street, tropical greenery vied for attention with the restlessly muttering pair of caged curved-beaked birds who obviously resented the subdued lights of wrought-iron lamps set to illuminate the way for evening diners. A trim-waisted young Mexican escorted them to a round table set for two in the high-ceilinged dining room which had possibly been an entrance hall in the days when the restaurant had been an exclusive mansion. *Piñon* logs burned in a vast open fireplace next to their table, chasing the evening chill and casting flickering shadows over each of their faces.

'What would you like to drink?' asked Román when the waiter came towards them.

'I'd like a *margarita*, please,' Laura requested, wishing as she glanced around at the gradually filling tables that she had worn something much more glamorous. Floating chiffon vied with straight thick satin in most of the other women diners, and she felt vastly underdressed in her white sleeveless shift that no more than delineated the woman's curves beneath it. She felt wisps of hair straggling towards her collar, and knew that her make-up had long since vanished.

'Will you excuse me?' she murmured, reaching for her bag as she rose, noting that Román politely got to his feet also. 'I won't be a moment.'

The moment stretched to several minutes as she repaired the ravages to her mouth and eyes and highlighted her cheekbones with brushed colour more suitable to the subdued lighting of the restaurant. As a final touch, she released her hair from its confining chignon and let it swirl around her face like burnished gold.

Román rose again when she returned to the table, his eyes sparkling approval when he said facetiously, 'So many artifices confined in such a small space!' It was obvious he referred to the bag she stuffed down beside her as she resumed her seat, but something about his freely roving glance told her that he appreciated the results of artifice rather than the means.

Sipping on the ice and fire of the *margarita* that had been delivered in her absence, she looked bemusedly at Román across the table. He was not, perhaps, dressed as formally as the other men in the room, but something about his aura suggested a vibrant oneness the other men lacked.

The white collar curving up and round his neck to outline the fine column of his throat acknowledged but made little of the virile, curling dark hair of his chest plainly visible between the folds of his shirt. Only his companion would be fully aware of his sensuous appeal, and Laura felt herself as vulnerable as a star-struck teenager would be in face of blatant male appeal to her senses.

'There are no menus to choose from,' he informed her, smiling. 'Soon a waiter will come and recite it, and we will have to choose what we want.'

'Oh.'

The question as to what she should have was solved instantly when the waiter drew up a stool and recited the evening's menu in Spanish in deference to Román, who was obviously expected to make the choice for both of them. This he did swiftly and without reference to Laura.

'You will enjoy the meal,' he informed her when the waiter had departed with his order. 'It is a mixture of Mexican dishes prepared with one eye on blander American tastes.'

And so it was. Laura helped herself to a mildly spicy dish of melted cheese which she spread on a toasting hot tortilla, adding a bare touch of the accompanying sauce before rolling the whole up into a thin oblong, and devouring it eagerly. Her appetite remained unabated while course followed course in the form of snippets of fish plumbed from the depths of the ocean not far from Guadalajara, the veal that melted in the mouth, and the fresh lemon pie she was unable to resist as a climax to the meal.

'*Café?*' enquired Román with a smile as she licked the dregs of the dessert spoon, and she hastily sat back in the high-laddered chair and blinked owlishly at Román, as if coming out of a singularly pleasant experience.

'Oh . . . yes, please.'

As if by magic, rich dark coffee materialised, and at the same time a waiter who had been serving another table came across to theirs and pulled up the stool their food waiter had used. The guitar in his hand was settled comfortably on his lap before he began to sing in a huskily meaningful voice, his dark eyes fastened soulfully on Laura's as he sang of the loneliness of unrequited love. Román's expression assumed an enigmatic cast as he leaned back and listened to the troubador's serenade to his partner. Nothing in the relaxed set of his jaw indicated anything other than detached interest in the evocative sensuality of the handsome young man's song, and when the last lingering notes died away, he reached into his pocket for a tip that made the singer thank him profusely before moving to the next table.

Laura felt a distinct sense of letdown . . . the liquid dark eyes and the husky tones had seemed meant for her alone, yet the plump matron at the next table was now receiving the same soulful concentration. A sigh of disillusionment brought Román's eyes up to gaze piercingly at her.

'If you are finished,' he suggested tactfully, 'we should perhaps find the car and go home.'

His light touch on her elbow as they left the restaurant sent soft waves of pleasure through her, and she mocked her own susceptibility to the

Mexican male's charm and air of leashed sensuality. It must be something about the climate, she reflected drily, that inspired this openness to romance. Deep in thought, she twisted her ankle on a cobblestone and Román instinctively reached an arm around her waist to draw her to him, leaving it there as they traversed the last block to the garage.

'Our wine can be very potent,' he remarked, a smile under his serious tone.

'I drank very little,' Laura protested indignantly. 'I should have worn more sensible shoes. Cobblestones weren't meant for narrow heels.'

'*Si*,' he agreed calmly, and pulled her by the hand up the stone steps to where the car was parked. Unlocking the passenger door first, he settled Laura into her seat before going round to get behind the wheel. The wine seemed not to have affected his driving judgment, and soon they were out of the narrow village streets and speeding back to the city along a thoroughfare that was still well peopled.

'Does no one ever sleep here?' Laura wondered aloud, and Román chuckled.

'The night is still young for Mexicans,' he said drily. 'We had an early dinner, remember.' His eyes glinted in the reflected glow of street lights as he slanted her a sideways look. 'Would you like to dance for a while before returning home?'

'Dance?'

'*Si*. We have several nightclubs in Guadalajara where one can dance between bouts of entertainment. Or are you, perhaps, too tired after visiting every shop in Tlaquepaque?' he ended on a slyly humorous note, and Laura wondered for a moment if he had been secretly bored with her tourist enthusiasm.

Faced with the prospect of her lonely room, she said impulsively, 'I'm not a bit tired, and I'd love to dance. Although,' she glanced ruefully down at her white shift dress, 'I'm really not dressed for a nightclub.'

Again he glanced at her, this time encompassing her from head to toe. 'Your appearance is acceptable to me,' he said coolly, and turned back dismissingly to his driving, leaving Laura shocked with this sudden reminder of his Latin male arrogance, his unquestioning assumption that what he found acceptable couldn't possibly be condemned by other, lesser persons. He was an anachronism in today's world, still living in a past where a man needed no more than a noble background to raise him above the level of average citizen.

Yet it wasn't only that quality in him that made him special, she mused honestly, her anger ebbing as she glanced surreptitiously at his darkened profile. Every hard line of his well-cut features expressed a man who would have carved a successful career for himself, however humble his background; he would never have settled for mediocrity.

Her hopes for a quietly inconspicuous table were dashed when they were greeted by the nightclub's manager himself and ushered to a ringside table next to where several couples were dancing on a sizeable oval dance floor. She should have known that Román would be offered nothing but the best wherever he went!

Drinks appeared like magic, brandy for Román

and the light white wine she had asked for, but he ignored their arrival and asked her politely to dance. However, the music stopped at that moment and the floor cleared when a drum-roll announced the live entertainment segment. Román grimaced and shrugged his shoulders.

'When this is over,' he murmured, then turned his head towards the bevy of young women dancers beginning their gyrations in the centre of the oval, while one more flamboyantly clothed took pride of place as the singer.

Laura had never considered herself unduly prudish, but somehow the sight of almost naked women undulating their red-gold flesh for the reward of catcalls and whistles from the males in the audience sent waves of hot embarrassment over her. How could Román have brought her to a place like this? A man who respected the woman he was with would surely be more selective—but perhaps he hadn't known himself.

One glance at his interestedly amused gaze as he leaned back in his chair, a faint smile on his mouth, told her he had known exactly what to expect, and humiliation mingled with the embarrassment heating her skin. Jerkily, she lifted her glass to sip at the wine and spilled a few drops on the white cloth, drawing Román's attention. He leaned forward.

'You are not enjoying the show, *Laura*?'

'I—guess I'm a little more tired than I thought,' she improvised hastily, 'and my head's beginning to ache.'

'Why did you not say so before, *pequeña*? We will leave at once.'

'No, please,' she glanced quickly round the

surrounding tables, knowing that leaving now would create a stir. 'Let's wait until this is over.'

His brows rose, the dark eyes under them giving her a piercing scrutiny that left her trembling, then finally he shrugged slightly and leaned back again in his chair. But he paid little more attention to the floorshow, adding guilt to Laura's discomfiture. Why couldn't she have been more devious about disguising her feelings? She had spoiled the end of an almost perfect day for both of them . . . and now there would be no dance, no way to know what it would be like to be held close by Román . . . and she was only now beginning to realise how much she had been looking forward to that. . .

Román rose as soon as the act ended and conducted her from the nightclub, pausing to exchange a few words with the manager, who was obviously anxious about the briefness of their visit. Outside, Laura drew a shaky breath and said in a small voice,

'Román, I'm sorry . . . I can take a taxi back if you'd rather stay longer.'

'*Dios!* You think I care about that kind of thing more than my responsibility to you? I simply thought you would enjoy a different experience, but you obviously did not, and I apologise if I offended you by taking you there.' His expression was haughtily remote as he handed her into the car, and Laura felt a flicker of apprehension.

'It seems *I've* offended *you*,' she said quietly when he got in beside her and started the motor, 'so I should be the one to apologise.'

He relaxed suddenly with his arms on the wheel and looked at her, baffled. 'You did offend

me, Laura, by telling me a lie about your
headache and being tired. Why could you not tell
me honestly that you did not like the show? I
would have understood.'

'Would you? You seemed to be enjoying it for
the same reasons I hated it.' She twisted her
hands together in her lap. 'You—all those men in
there—were making sexual objects of those
women, degrading them. . .'

Román remained quiet for several moments,
then, sighing, he straightened and moved the car
forward, saying, 'In my experience, no woman is
ever exploited sexually except by her own wish.
Those women enjoy what they do, what they
inspire, or they would not be there.'

'They have to work for their living, surely?'
Laura pointed out heatedly, discretion forgotten,
and Román threw his head back to laugh
cynically.

'Oh, come, Laura, you don't believe there is no
other choice open to them? They could be
typists, store clerks, even wives if their in-
clinations led them that way. Obviously they do
not.'

Frustrated in her argument, though still feeling
she was right, Laura subsided into a chilly
silence, which Román broke almost immediately.

'Did your lover not teach you that sexual
feelings are good, whatever inspires them?' he
asked softly.

'M-my lover?' Laura blinked and stared at his
averted profile for several moments before
realising what he meant. 'Gavin wasn't my lover!'
she denied vehemently.

'No?'

'No!'

'Ah.' The quiet satisfaction in his voice had her blinking again, but they were turning into the opened gates of the Villa Castillo, so there was no time to vent her wrath at his sly probing that had uncovered a truth she would rather have kept to herself . . . being a virgin at almost twenty-three made her as anachronistic as he with his antiquated standards. Still, she thought as she stepped from the car, he wasn't to know there hadn't been others apart from Gavin.

Lights had been left on in the hall and both staircases, and Laura kept her voice low when she paused in the centre beside the quiescent fountain to thank Román formally for the day.

'It's been wonderful, Román, thank you.' Not knowing what else to do to finalise the evening, she held out her hand and felt his fingers immediately slide over it, though not to shake it. Instead he used it to pull her forward towards him, his smile lazily quizzical as he said softly,

'Our day together is not over yet, Laura. We have not yet had the dance we promised each other.'

'Dance?' They were standing so close that she had to angle her head up to gaze, puzzled, into the warm gleam far back in his eyes. A tremor started in her knees and shivered its way up to where her body lightly touched the hard surface of his, so that he couldn't fail to recognise the effect he was having on her. 'Here?—now?' Even her voice held a shakiness she was powerless to control, and she bit down on her lower lip in vexation. He was the last man in the world she would reveal her feelings to, even if she were madly in love with him. The proud arrogance in his nature would turn that kind of knowledge into a weapon he wouldn't hesitate to use over her. Or any woman. . .

Rapid as her thoughts had been, she still missed his murmured reply, and rather than ask him to repeat it she let herself be tugged gently towards the staircase leading to his private quarters. A protest rose and died in her throat. If she made a scene about it, it would make her appear a lot less mature than she prided herself on being . . . more than that, he would assume she was afraid to be alone with him.

His hand lightly on her waist now to propel her forward into the ultra-sophistication of his living room, Román grimaced at the brightness of the lights which, presumably, a servant had left on for his return. Reaching his free hand to a switch close to the door, he pressed it and immediately the glare dimmed to the rosy warmth of a few strategically placed sidelamps.

'Manuel is in constant fear that my eyes will suddenly fail me,' he remarked wryly, waving a hand towards the chintz-covered sofas that formed the seating area and moving easily across to an exquisitely carved Provincial cabinet which he opened to reveal a neatly arranged bar. 'Will you have a nightcap, Laura?'

Again, it would have seemed less than sophisticated to refuse, so she thanked him coolly and walked nonchalantly to a corner of one of the sofas, dropping her purse on the cushion next to hers as she sat down. She would probably have taken a solitary armchair if there had been one, but then that would have proved—irritated by

her own sensitivity, she frowned and watched
his economical movements at the bar. What in
the world could happen to her, here in the Villa
Castillo where a scream would bring a flock of
people running? The thought struck her as
humorous somehow, and she was smiling
slightly when Román walked over with the
drinks, placing hers on the side table by her
corner and taking his own to the other end,
where he settled himself comfortably and raised
one brow at her.

'I am glad to find you more relaxed now,
Laura. What did you think, that I brought you
up here to ravage you?' His tone was lightly
amused, but Laura sensed an edge to it.

'Of course not,' she tried to match his tone and
failed. 'You'd hardly do that in your own home,
would you?'

'But you think I might somewhere else?' His
eyes had narrowed suddenly and his features took
on the remote, proud look she was beginning to
recognise.

'No,' she said quietly, 'I imagine you don't
have to do that where women are concerned.'

He seemed surprised by her candour, his eyes
fully open as he regarded her from his corner
position. 'That's true,' he admitted evenly, 'but I
would never in any case take what was given
reluctantly.'

Laura could think of nothing to say in reply to
a statement like that, so she picked up her drink
and gulped thirstily, almost choking when she
discovered it was her least favourite, brandy,
although well diluted with soda. But perhaps it
was what she needed to meet a situation like this.

The second sip went down smoothly and sent a relaxing warmth into her limbs.

'Is the drink too strong for you?' Román made her aware that he had been watching her reactions, and she shook her head.

'It's fine.'

Into the strained silence that fell between them, Román asked quietly, 'Why are you so afraid of me, Laura? It was not so today when we walked together in Tlaquepaque.' Holding hands, his unspoken ending implied, and Laura shifted restlessly after replacing her glass on the side table.

'Why should I be afraid of you?'

He shrugged. 'I only know that you are, and it—concerns me. I had thought we were becoming good friends, but now you put up a barrier between us. Why is this?'

Laura attempted a dismissing laugh, but it came out more as a strangled squeak than anything. 'You're imagining things—I'm not in the least afraid of you. If I seem so, then it must be because I'm tired after a long day. And, speaking of that,' she got to her feet and leaned back to pick up her bag, 'will you excuse me if I leave now? I really am tired.' This time it was no lie; her eyes felt enormously large and over-bright, and the brandy had only succeeded in accentuating the lethargy in her body.

'I will excuse you after we have danced,' Román insisted levelly, rising too and walking with animal smoothness to a stereo set she hadn't noticed before set into an alcove close to the bar.

Laura stood frozen to the spot, fighting down an overwhelming sense of panic, realising how untrue her statement had been. She *was* afraid of him . . . not in a physical sense, but because of the attraction she had felt for him from the moment she had looked up from his desk and saw him for the first time. He stood for everything her independent spirit spurned, and it would be madness to indulge a passing fancy for a man who happened to resemble the fictitious hero of her new book to the last degree. Yet when he turned from the stereo and held out his arms and said, 'Come,' she went towards him like a prisoner numbed at the prospect of facing the firing squad at last.

The music he had selected was soft, dreamy, tugging at her crumbling defences as their steps fitted awkwardly at first, then settled into an easy rhythm that required no effort to follow. It was as if they had danced together many times before, each anticipating the other's movements with the sixth sense of familiarity. The warm hard outline of his body against hers was somehow achingly familiar too, the feel of constriction in her breasts as his chest pressed harshly against them, the taut lines of his thighs on the soft firmness of hers as they guided her round the smooth marble floor. There was familiarity, too, in the fluttering waves of excitement that spread warm fingers to reach every last part of her, robbing her of breath so that she made no effort to resist when one of Román's hands came up from supporting her back to gently nudge her cheek against the head he had stooped towards her.

'Laura,' he muttered thickly, nuzzling with his lips against her still-cool skin, 'how beautiful you are, and so sweetly innocent. You set my blood on fire with desire for you, yet,' he raised his head and looked with sensually lidded eyes into hers, 'the wonderful blue of your eyes seeks always to cool my passion. Don't do it now, *por favor*, or my blood will burst from its vessels!'

The hotly passionate, overly dramatic words served to bring a measure of sanity back into Laura's swimming senses, but the faint smile beginning to light her eyes faded when her gaze was drawn to the tautly stretched olive skin across his high cheekbones, the proud line of his hawklike nose, the forceful jut of his chin, shaded blue-black for want of a shave ... a strange hunger filled her when her gaze lifted to the sensual curve of his mouth and lingered there while pulses she hadn't been aware of pounded thickly in her veins.

'Román, I——' she began in a whisper, not knowing whether she protested or invited, and then suddenly it didn't matter any more, because he bent his head a little further and placed his mouth on hers, scattering what remained of her senses as he kissed her gently at first, then with a rising force of passion that had her clinging helplessly to the muscled lines of his shoulders. Her hands searched independently for the cool soft thickness of hair at his nape, knowing it would feel just that way.

His hand circled her throat slowly and stroked the soft line of her underjaw before dipping confidently to the soft swell of her breasts under the loose confinement of her dress. His breath was drawn in raggedly as he lifted his mouth from hers and fired her skin with searing kisses that burned from mouth to throat and stole her breath away again. A wild kind of pride coursed through her that she possessed the ability to inflame the passions of a man like Román Castillo, who could have his choice of any beauty in Mexico.

In the next instant she realised with cold, clear clarity that he *had* had his choice of beauties, and would continue to do so once the novelty of her newness wore off. No woman, even a wife— *especially* a wife—would hold him longer than it took for familiarity to set in.

The thought was mother to the action, and she stiffened against him before wrenching herself from the arms she had welcomed moments before. A pang of regret—or was it sorrow?—shot through her when she saw the look of stunned disbelief in his passion-glazed eyes.

'Laura? What——?'

'I'm sorry if I misled you, *señor*,' she said on a breathless note of irony, 'but I'm not available for one of your casual affairs, so if you'll excuse me. . .'

An oath she had never heard him use burst from his lips and his hand shot out to swing her back towards him when she turned with dignity to leave.

'What are you saying?' he asked roughly, his eyes like hot coals as they raked over her face. 'You think I want you for a night or two, a month or two? I had hoped to lead up to it after a proper period of courtship, but you force me to speak my mind at this early stage in our relationship. I do not want you as a temporary lover, Laura . . . I want you for my wife.'

CHAPTER SIX

LAURA stared at him with eyes she knew were bulging unattractively, but her state of shock was so great that she could do nothing about it. *Marry* him, was that what he had said? Under other circumstances the thought would have been ludicrous, but something about Román's stark look, the pallor underlying his olive skin, pointed up the seriousness of his proposal.

She sent a moistening tongue over her lips. 'You—you hardly know me, *señor*, yet you ask me to marry you?'

'I know enough about you to recognise that you will be an excellent wife for me,' he dismissed loftily. 'The mother of my children must be above reproach, and I believe you to be that.'

'The mother——?' Laura stared at him disbelievingly, knowing that she was living through a particularly exotic dream but unable to wake herself from it. 'Don't people have to be in love before they marry and have children?' she resorted to irony.

'We are attracted to each other,' his shoulders lifted in a dismissing shrug, 'and that is a sufficient foundation to build a good marriage on.' His fingers raked through the hair her own had smoothed passionately minutes before, a vulnerable gesture that somehow touched her.

'I'm sorry, Román,' her tone gentled, 'I'm just

not used to the Latin way of doing things, I guess. In my country we fall in love with a man before committing ourselves to marriage.'

'But you are not indifferent to me?' he asked with irrefutable logic, considering her response to his lovemaking, and she coloured in embarrassment, only now becoming aware of the long-playing record that still emitted romantic strains into the cosily lit room.

'No, of course not,' she said desperately, feeling caught in a web that moment by moment wound itself more tightly around her. 'But there's a big difference between being attracted to someone and wanting to spend the rest of your life with him! Marriage in my country means—well, a commitment to each other, a loyalty to that commitment——'

'And if I promised this loyalty to the cold-blooded commitment you speak of,' he interrupted harshly, 'you would consider marrying me?'

'If I loved you, yes,' she agreed, agonised by the futility of it all.

'Then I will devote my life to making you love me,' he said decisively, as if the task presented no problem at all—which it probably didn't under normal circumstances, Laura thought despairingly. 'Meantime, *chica*,' his voice softened protectively, 'you need your rest. I will escort you back to your room.'

Despite her protests, he did just that, and bade her goodnight with a kiss on the lips that was already possessive to her thinking. Trembling in after-reaction, she leaned back against the door she had closed in his face and tried to gather her scattered thoughts. The whole situation was ludicrous, like something from a nineteenth-century novel that had no connection with the twentieth-century world. A man who was an admitted womaniser wanted her for his wife ... why? ... why?

Laura moved further into the room and began to remove her clothes, her brow furrowed in perplexity. And the answer hit her, so suddenly that her hand stilled on the zipper of her dress. Of course ... he had discovered in his probing that she was untouched in a sexual way—a fitting mother for the heirs to the Castillo dynasty! Román considered himself the equal of European royalty, his children having the same immunity from questionable origins as theirs did. It was archaic, ridiculous in today's world, but she knew instinctively that this was the way his mind worked.

As for fidelity, his promise was as meaningless as subterfuge could make it. Like the heroine of her novel, Maria Delgado, she would never know for sure how many mistresses occupied his free hours, but she would be aware of them in the way a woman in love with her husband was aware of his extra-marital interests.

Laura quickly finished undressing and slid her nightdress over her head before going into the palatial bathroom to rinse her face and hands and clean her teeth. She had the advantage over poor Maria Delgado ... she wasn't in love with the man who sought to be her husband. Attracted to him, yes, but there was nothing irrevocable in her feelings towards him. She would make her apologies to Isabel for the shortness of her visit and beat a hasty retreat from the Villa Castillo.

Even without Román's promised historic documentation, she had more than enough information to at least get started on her book. . .

A night spent in restless sleep left Laura feeling pale and washed out when morning came. The decision she had made the night before to leave the Villa Castillo should have brought some measure of peace, but it hadn't. She had been too conscious of the new feelings that had been stirred in her mind and body, too aware that the man who had provoked those feelings slept only the courtyard's distance away.

Or had he lain awake too, staring at a darkened ceiling, regretting his impulsive proposal of marriage to a woman he scarcely knew, a woman whose background in no way matched his? No, she answered herself sourly, throwing back the covers and dragging herself to the bathroom for a quick, cool shower. He wasn't the kind to make hasty decisions like that, not when it involved bestowing the honour of his name on the future mother of his children!

Gasping as the cool water struck her warm skin, she began to soap herself hurriedly. 'Román must have laid his plans years ago, meticulously plotted the course of his private life. So many years of bachelor freedom, a certain age to marry an appropriately pure girl of good family . . . she didn't have to be wealthy, he had more than enough assets to support them in his accustomed style.

Rinsing, then towelling herself roughly, she reflected drily that his proposal hadn't been that much of a compliment; any suitable woman would do, provided she appeared in his life at the right time. How typical of his Latin temperament to make the woman's willingness his least concern! And how shocked he would be to discover that there was at least one woman in the world he couldn't manipulate with his wealth, his noble ancestry, his good looks, his expertise in lovemaking.

Wandering back into the bedroom to dress, she felt a glow that had nothing to do with the cool shower spreading across her face. She could never argue with that last quality of his; the memory of her own reactions had kept her tossing and turning most of the night. She had always felt slightly detached in her amorous encounters with men, coolly amused by friends and books that described thrills and raptures that carried away to self-forgetfulness. Last night, for the first time, she knew what they had meant. Mortified as she was now to admit it, there had been a point when Román could have manipulated her to his will, even to taking her to the high canopied bed in the next room and. . .

Rosa knocked lightly and came in with the breakfast tray, seeming surprised to see that Laura was already dressed for the day. 'You are going out early, *señorita?*'

'No, I—yes, perhaps,' Laura hesitated, then, 'Rosa, would you please tell Señora Isabel that I would like to see her as soon as possible? I have something important to tell her.'

'*Sí, señorita.*'

Laura went slowly to the balcony doors, a cup of steaming coffee in her hand, and glanced down into the courtyard. For once, the day was cloudy

and threatening rain . . . the plants would enjoy a
refreshing shower, even the flame tree's blossoms
were drooping a little. Her gaze sharpened when
a figure emerged from under the patio overhang
and her heart lurched and began to beat
flutteringly in her breast. She was shocked by the
disappointment that flooded over her when she
recognised the gardener. Only then did she
acknowledge that she had been waiting for a
glimpse of Román's lithe stride, the frown of
preoccupation on his darkly good-looking features
telling her that his thoughts were already in his
office coping with the first of the day's problems.

She swung so violently from the window that
coffee splashed into the saucer. Almost angrily
she replaced it on the tray and decided against
pouring more for the moment. It was perfectly
natural, wasn't it, that she should want a last
glimpse of the man who had been her host in
Guadalajara?' Regardless of how she felt about
him now, she owed him at least a small debt of
gratitude.

Was she being cowardly in leaving without
seeing him again? Surely not; he was sensitive
enough to know immediately her reason for
leaving so hurriedly. Seeing him in person would
be painful for both of them, perhaps him most of
all.

It was an hour later, and Laura had already
begun to stack her novel notes preparatory to
packing them, when Rosa tapped again and put
her head around the half-open door. 'The Señora
will see you at once in the small *sala, señorita*.
She is very excited, and says you must hurry.'

Laura nodded, then stared blankly at the door

Rosa closed behind her. How could Isabel possibly have known of her plans to leave that day? That was the only reason Laura could think of for excitement on the older woman's part, and she felt a pang of compunction as she ran down the stairs holding lightly to the banister. In view of her innocuous position in the household, Isabel had been more than generous in offering her accommodation in the Villa Castillo.

Laura was frowning slightly when she walked rapidly towards the small sitting room, pausing in shock on the threshold when she took in not only a plumply smiling Isabel, standing by a small table facing the door and holding a letter in her hand, but a dark-suited Román who also looked quietly pleased about something. The thought flashed through her mind that perhaps it had been he who had guessed that she would fly the coop and that the thought had relieved him of any commitment to his hasty offer of last night.

Isabel, surprisingly still dressed in a bedroom robe, fluttered towards her with arms out-stretched, her smile changing to a beam that made her dark eyes sparkle.

'Ah, Laura, how happy you have made me this morning! I could not wait to tell you!' She kissed Laura effusively on both cheeks, then held her away and looked at her roguishly. 'I must say, I had not expected it to happen so soon, but then you young people today make up your minds so quickly! I knew, of course, as soon as I got your message that you had something to tell me that it must be something like this, and Román confirmed my suspicions.'

Stunned, Laura looked at Román, whose

expression had amazingly changed to one of mild
reproach. It was as if she walked into a
nightmarish dream where no one was acting as
they should. Now Román was walking towards
her, lifting her hand and pressing his lips to her
fingers in a slow, meaningful way.

'I would have preferred that I be the first one
informed of your decision, *querida*,' he murmured
huskily, 'but the most important fact, after all, is
that you have consented to be my wife.'

Laura felt the colour drain from her face, leaving
it stiff and unpliable. This *must* be a nightmare!
How could her message to Isabel possibly have
been interpreted as an agreement to marriage?
Her brain felt numb as if the blood had ebbed
from that too, and she stared in bewilderment at
Isabel as she prattled on again.

'And this letter,' she waved a vaguely familiar
notepaper before Laura's stunned eyes, 'so much
excitement in one day! If it had been planned to
the last detail, it could not have worked out
better.'

Laura licked her dry lips and said hoarsely,
'What—couldn't have worked out better?'

'Why, the visit of your parents, of course! Oh,
forgive me, my dear,' Isabel smote her brow with
the letter in question, 'I forgot that you did not
know of that yet. There is a letter for you, too,
from your mother, no doubt telling you the same
things. She and your father are being sent away
to—oh, somewhere—and they want to see you,
naturally, before they leave.'

Laura's sense of unreality deepened. Her
parents, coming here? Dazedly, she wondered

why they would do that when she was going back to the States today. Román still held her hand, between them now, and she instinctively clung to the calming strength emanating from his fingers. Only vaguely did she hear Isabel's excited laying of plans.

'Perhaps we can persuade them to stay longer than the two weeks they suggest—three or four weeks would give me time to arrange the wedding. Would it not be wonderful, Laura, to have them here when you are married? I would see to all the arrangements, of course,' she added jealously, 'since you will be married from this house.'

It was all suddenly too much for Laura. 'Please,' she begged faintly, words freezing in her throat and making it impossible for her to voice them.

Then Román was speaking in that intimately husky voice again, muffled further by his gesture of once more pressing his lips to her hand. 'I am devastated, *mi novia*, to have to leave you so soon after our happiness has begun, but there is a very important meeting I must attend this morning. Tonight we dine, just you and I, together.'

Laura stared desperately after him, wanting to call him back, but his rapid stride had carried him out of sight across the hall before she could articulate even a strangled moan.

'Ah, how sweet, already you are sad at parting from him,' Isabel crooned sickeningly, taking Laura's arm and leading her to the comfortable armchairs set around the fireplace. 'Come, my dear, and we will make plans for the wedding and you will not feel so sad. Now,' she settled herself in her usual chair and looked brightly at Laura, who stared distractedly back at her without seeing the avid excitement in the older woman's face. 'It is fortunate that you are of our religion, so much time will be saved as you will not have to take instruction.' She frowned. 'It will be difficult—well, unusual, to have the reception at the Villa Castillo as it is not strictly speaking your home, but then,' her expression brightened, 'it will have been your home for some weeks by the time of the ceremony, will it not? The wedding dress—I think I can persuade my dressmaker to work quickly on it, she——'

'What is all this talk about wedding dresses and dressmakers, Mamá?' asked Nicolas in a baffled voice from the doorway. 'Are you marrying old Sánchez after all?'

Isabel twisted in her chair to look abstractedly at him, as if he were a stranger. 'Certainly not, Nico,' she denied hotly, adding illogically, 'and if I were marrying him I would not need the kind of wedding dress I am thinking of for Laura.'

'*Laura!*'

Nicolas looked as stunned as Laura felt.

'Yes, Laura,' his mother replied testily, resenting his intrusion into her lovely world of planning. 'She and Román are to be married as soon as it can be arranged.'

'*Román!*'

'Please do not repeat everything I say in that amazed voice, Nicolas,' she commanded loftily. 'What is so surprising about your cousin marrying this beautiful guest of ours? Come and wish her well, instead of standing there with your mouth open!'

Nicolas did move slowly forward, but by the time he reached Laura there was a cynical twist on his softly shaped mouth. 'I congratulate you, Laura, on landing my wily cousin so quickly,' he sneered. 'As for luck, you will need lots of it if you marry Román. He is rigid in his requirements for his employees, and he will be even more so in regard to his wife's behaviour.'

'*Nicolas!*' Isabel was plainly furious, but her son simply smiled his disdain.

'You know it is true, Mamá. Look at how he treats me, his own cousin!'

'Marriage to Laura will soften him,' Isabel predicted with certainty. 'A man without a wife is like a plum that never ripens sweetly, you will see.'

Ignoring that, Nicolas perched on the arm of a chair and directed his attention to Laura again, curiosity sharpening his brown-eyed gaze. 'You know very little about my cousin, Laura, how could you in such a short time? You have never seen his famous temper in action, have you? It is formidable, I assure you. I tell you this to help you in your relations with him. Never cross him, or he will destroy you.'

From somewhere, Laura found the words to match his insolence. 'He hasn't yet destroyed you, although I believe you cross him quite frequently.' It was only later, in the privacy of her room, that she realised she had taken a defensive stand on Román's behalf . . . as a true fiancée would have.

'I must go,' Nicolas stood up abruptly, a dull red flush darkening his pale olive skin, 'or your lover will have another excuse for flying into a

temper. Goodbye, Mamá, Laura.' He stalked
from the room, and Isabel glanced appealingly at
Laura.

'You must forgive him, Laura, he is still young
and more interested in the pleasures of life than
in business. But that will change as he grows
older and realises his responsibilities. Román
does not recognise this yet, but I am sure your
understanding will help him to be less harsh with
Nico. Sometimes,' she ended thoughtfully, 'I think
Román has a feeling of guilt that the family
businesses were left solely to him. Perhaps this is
why he is so hard with Nico.'

With a sense of shock, Laura realised that
Isabel was enlisting her in the constant war
between Román and Nicolas . . . as if she had any
influence with Román!

'Well, let us get back to our plans,' Isabel
rushed on, looking startled when Laura rose
suddenly to her feet.

'Will you forgive if I go back to my room now?
I have a headache coming on, and——'

'Ah, of course,' Isabel nodded understandingly,
rising too, 'so much excitement so quickly. Oh,'
she darted to the table where she had dropped the
letter she had received from Eleanor, 'here is the
letter from your mother. Why don't you rest on
your bed and read it?'

Laura gave her a slight, ironic smile as she took
the familiar green airmail envelope from her
hostess . . . at this rate, Isabel would have her
reduced to a state of helpless dependency, unable
to think for herself. She had already let herself be
bulldozed into the belief that she would marry
Román, she reflected dully as she ascended the

stairs to the upper floor. Why hadn't she made her protests, denials, as soon as she realised the situation? A woman of twenty-three in today's world didn't stand meekly by while others arranged her future for her.

Entering her room, she tossed her mother's letter on the night-table and lay on top of the bed, which Rosa had already made up to smooth neatness. Clasping her hands behind her head, she stared up at the ceiling which had been obscured in her wakefulness during the night. *Why* hadn't she made a definite correction when Isabel and Román greeted her with their false assumption? Because she couldn't bear to see Isabel's face fall in disappointment? Hardly. A person didn't sacrifice her future for the sake of a well-meaning older woman. Because Román had looked so quietly, deeply happy?

Laura disengaged the hand he had held to kiss and stared at it as if she had never seen it before. Its past, present and future held only one impression for her ... the warm touch of Román's lips on its skin, and the secondary one of her own fingers clasping tightly to his for the strength she needed in a bad moment.

Her eyes grew mistily thoughtful as she stared at her hand. It wasn't possible to fall in love so quickly with a man whose outdated principles clashed so discordantly with one's own ... was it?

A tap at the door startled her into wakefulness, and she stared owlishly at Rosa as she advanced into the room and placed a large tray on the round table at the seating area.

'I am sorry to wake you, *señorita*,' she said

softly, 'but Señora Isabel was afraid you would
be hungry. I have brought *comida* for you, since
the Señora ate an hour ago.'

'Oh.' Laura struggled to an upright position
and looked at her watch. Two-thirty! 'I didn't
mean to sleep at all, let alone for four hours!
Thank you, Rosa.'

The maid smiled shyly. 'Today is very exciting
for you, *señorita*. We are all very happy that you
and Don Román are going to be married.'

Laura groaned inwardly. Not the servants
too! For several hours she had floated on a gentle
sea of oblivion that had left her only warm
feelings of contentment, and now she was
plunged headlong back into the confusion of her
waking thoughts.

'Er—thank you, Rosa.' And thank you, Isabel,
she added mentally, for spreading the happy
tidings! Probably at this moment she was
gabbling the news to her friends all over town,
having forgone her siesta in honour of the
occasion. As Rosa smiled again and left the room,
she swung her legs over the side of the bed and
ran a distracted hand through her tousled hair.
What was she to do? This farce couldn't go on.
She felt like a ball someone had picked up and
run with to the next base, no time to draw her
breath before being hurried to the next. It all
made her feel somewhat detached, numb, as if it
were happening to someone else.

She was surprised to find, on approaching the
tray Rosa had deposited, that the aromas rising
from the covered dishes whetted her appetite to
eagerness, but then she remembered that she had
eaten nothing for breakfast. She sat down and

savoured every scrap of the tender veal in rich wine sauce, the tiny potatoes drenched with parsley butter, the pale green stalks of asparagus, finishing off with the colourful fresh fruit *compôte*. Replete, she carried her coffee to the balcony table and saw that the promised shower had occurred, although the sun was once more shining in a deep blue sky.

Remembering suddenly that she hadn't yet read her mother's letter, she hurried back inside and tore the envelope flap open as she walked back to the balcony. The sight of her mother's freely looped handwriting sent a sudden sting of tears to her eyes.

'Darling Laura,' she read, 'I know it will come as a surprise to you to hear that Dad and I are planning a visit to Mexico very soon—in fact, we'll be arriving a few days after you receive this! We've just heard that our last assignment overseas is to Paris again, so you can imagine how happy we are about that, seeing old friends, etc. But we couldn't go without spending a little time with you in Mexico. I'm writing to Isabel too, but don't anticipate any problems there as she's always asking us to come. Do hope your book is coming along. . .'

Laura dropped the letter on the table and focused hazily on the refreshed blossoms of the flame tree. What would her parents think of the predicament she had inadvertently brought upon herself? Her father would be bluntly direct in telling her she should have made the situation clear as soon as the error arose; her mother?

Eleanor would see the humorous side of it, as she always did. It would amuse her mightily that the daughter whom she loved dearly but always regarded as slightly on the sober side had embroiled herself in such a farcical situation.

Laura leaned her head on her hands and stared moodily at the coffee she had barely touched. Why did they have to choose now of all times to come? If the letter had arrived a day later she would have been back in the States, and there would be no need for them to come to Mexico. Her spine stiffened, lifting her head. She could telephone them, tell them she had planned to come home for Christmas, that the notes for the book were complete. Yes, of course, why hadn't she thought of that? They need never know that Román Castillo existed, let alone that he had assumed their daughter had agreed to marry him.

She had reckoned without the volatile Isabel. Having spent the afternoon working in desultory fashion on her book, Laura took a leisurely bath to release the tension that had tied her muscles in knots, and took her time about choosing what to wear for the evening. Román's pride was such that he would be mortally offended if she blurted out in front of his aunt, and perhaps Nicolas, that he had made a mistake. She would go to dinner with him and tell him then, privately. With that thought in mind, she selected her black dress with long, puffed chiffon sleeves as being suitably serious for the occasion. Her hair, too, was arranged in a severe style, only a few red-gold strands escaping from the tightly drawn back chignon to add a softening touch. The diamond and sapphire bracelet and earrings her parents had given her for her twenty-first birthday were more elaborate than she would have preferred, but she owned nothing more suitable.

Román was crossing the hall from his own staircase when she started down hers, and he halted suddenly when he caught sight of her. His involuntary 'Dios!' floated up to her, and she tried desperately to control the hammer of her heartbeat as she stepped with her natural grace down the long curve of the staircase. Román had recovered his equilibrium and moved forward to meet her when she reached the bottom, his eyes like liquid flame as they devoured every inch of her. His touch was somehow reverent when he raised her hand to his lips for the inevitable kiss.

'I do not deserve such beauty,' he murmured with a humbleness that amazed her, 'but I will always cherish it, I promise.'

Laura almost succumbed to the treachery of tears, but reminded herself in time that the whole situation was false. Nevertheless, her voice held a nervously louder ring to it than she had intended.

'I'd like to phone my parents before we leave, if you don't mind,' she gestured to the instrument sitting squatly on an antique table under the curve of the stairs.

'What a wonderful idea!' exclaimed Isabel, hurrying out from the small *sala* bedecked in harsh magenta-coloured chiffon with panels that floated around her as she walked. 'We will all talk to them . . . I want to tell Eleanor that she and your father are very welcome at the Villa Castillo—and you, Román,' she turned officiously to her nephew, 'should speak to Laura's father.'

'I had intended to do so, Tia Isabel,' he sounded amused, 'but face to face, when I ask him for his daughter in marriage.'

'No, no, no, you must speak to him now, and then again when he comes. Do you want him to think we are savages with no idea of how to behave?'

Feeling herself again carried along on a relentless wave, Laura followed Isabel to the library, where the call could be made in greater comfort. There was no possibility of conversing with her parents privately, what with Isabel breathing down her neck and Román standing alertly a few paces away. Her finger trembled as it dialled direct to her parents' number in Washington.

'They must be out,' she said, betraying her relief in her voice. At the last moment, just as she was about to replace the receiver, the ringing stopped and there was a breathless 'Hello' at the other end. Eleanor.

'Oh darling, how nice to hear your voice! We were just on our way out, but you know how I can never resist answering a ringing telephone. How are you, did you get my letter?'

'Yes, I—I got it. Mother, I——'

'We're both looking forward so much to seeing you,' her mother rushed on, 'and if it's all right with Isabel, we can stay on over Christmas. What with Mike being away and it being a family time—heaven knows when we'll see you again, the Paris job might last as long as four years——'

'Mother, I have to tell you——'

'Is Isabel there? If so, put her on and I'll ask her myself,' Eleanor interrupted again breezily,

and Laura gave up, handing the phone silently to
the avid Isabel, who grasped it and in her
excitement spoke with a more pronounced accent
than usual.

'Eleanor, *cara*!' After an exchange of greetings,
she frowned and then beamed delightedly. 'But
of course it is all right for you to come and stay as
long as you want. In fact, I had hoped to
persuade you to stay on for the wedding . . . Ah,
I forgot,' she said regretfully, 'you do not yet
know that Laura and my nephew, Román, have
today decided to be married . . . yes, it is true.'
She listened for a moment, then put her hand
over the mouthpiece to hiss to Laura, 'She says
why did you not mention this when you were
talking to her?'

Because I didn't have the chance to say
anything, Laura responded silently, resentfully,
but before she could articulate the words Román
stepped forward and took the telephone decisively
from his aunt's hand.

What he said remained a blur in Laura's
memory, her thoughts too inner-orientated to
grasp anything other than the effect his attractively accented voice would be having on her
mother. Always aware of male appeal, despite her
devotion to her husband, Eleanor would be
completely bowled over by the romance of it all.
If only it had been her father who had answered
the phone! He would have known in a minute
that something was amiss in his daughter's
hesitant voice, but evidently he was waiting
impatiently for his wife in the car drawn up
outside their Georgetown residence.

'Then we will look forward to seeing you two

days from now,' Román was saying politely, 'and I will speak with your husband then.' Before Laura had a chance to re-enter the conversation with her mother, he had replaced the receiver and turned with quietly satisfied eyes to her. 'Your mother sounds a warm person, and very happy that her daughter has found her future in Mexico!'

Darn Eleanor, and her susceptibility to an attractive Latin accent! How could she possibly believe that her daughter had fallen madly in love in a matter of days with a man so alien to her own background and way of thinking? Couldn't she have insisted on speaking to her daughter again in spite of her husband's impatience to be gone to whatever function called them? Seething inside, she numbly accepted Román's fingers at her elbow as he guided her out into the hall. This whole state of affairs had gone far enough. Over dinner, she would make it clear to him that she had no intention of marrying him, in two weeks or four weeks or ever.

CHAPTER SEVEN

LAURA watched the silver plane with its distinctive markings land like an ungainly bird on the ribbon of runway, nodding when Román's fingers pressed on her arm to tell her it was time to go below to greet her parents.

Eyes of strangers looked curiously at the slender American redhead accompanied by the attentive and arresting figure of the Mexican man whose touch never strayed from her elbow as they went down to the lower area to greet her parents. Laura was oblivious to the stares, her heart beating erratically under the greenish blue of her skirt suit. What she had been unable to do for herself, they would surely accomplish, she thought with a cowardice alien to her free spirit.

It had been cowardice not to nip Román's erroneous assumption in the bud, she had acknowledged freely over the past few days; cowardice to let herself face the true facts when his undeniably attractive person had made restrained love to her.

'I would like to take you to my bed now,' he had admitted simply on their return to the Villa Castillo that night of the phone call to her parents, 'but I will not. We have many years ahead of us to become the lovers we were destined to be.'

Lovers. Destiny. Both were alien concepts to

Laura, who longed only to be free again, a woman making choices as to the disposition of her future. Yet she had found it impossible to assert her independence from Román . . . perhaps because the feminine part of her thrilled to the touch of his cool, dry skin, the restrained passion in the lips he applied often to her hand, to the lips she held rigidly when his mouth demanded hers. She had set a limit on her acquiescence . . . now, that limit had been reached with the arrival of her parents.

She saw Eleanor first, recognising the apple green she favoured in the well-cut skirt suit that emphasised a figure still attractive to men. Seconds later, her father hove into view, and tears stung her eyes as they took in the tall, casually dressed figure that loomed over her mother's. His eyes swept impersonally round the entrance hall and lit up when they alighted on his daughter. His arm lifted in a salute, and Laura stepped closer to the barrier to greet them.

'Darling, you look pale,' her mother remarked before pressing her cheek to Laura's, stepping back to let her husband envelop his daughter in a bear-hug that brought tears to her eyes. 'And you must be Román,' Eleanor fastened inspecting eyes on the man who stood at Laura's side. 'I was a little worried to know that Laura had made up her mind so quickly about the man she wanted to marry,' she said breathlessly, 'but now I see why. How do you do, Román?'

His reply was lost to Laura as she clung emotionally to her father, who finally thrust her from him and declared, 'If being engaged makes you this affectionate, kitten, I'm all for it!' His handshake with Román was forthright and shrewdly assessing in the sharpness of his blue eyes that so closely resembled Laura's. 'This young woman is very important to us,' he informed the politely smiling Román, 'so be sure you take good care of her.'

Laura could have screamed at her parent's acceptance of the status quo, but Román just dipped his head in acquiescence as he gripped the old man's hand.

'I can freely promise that her life will always mean more to me than my own,' he murmured with Latin emotionalism which her father amazingly accepted at face value.

'Good, good.' His eyes strayed round the entrance lobby. 'If we can get someone to carry our bags,' he suggested, 'we can get out of here.'

Román flicked his fingers once and Manuel, accompanied by a gardener's helper at the Villa Castillo, came forward to relieve the Bensons of their luggage. 'The car is waiting outside,' he added smoothly, touching his fingers to Laura's elbow again as they moved forward towards the exit. 'My aunt is looking forward to greeting you at the Villa Castillo.'

'It's been so long since I met Isabel,' remarked Eleanor as she settled herself on the grey upholstery beside Laura, the men taking their places on the pull-down seats opposite, 'that I'm not sure I'll recognise her now.'

'She has changed very little over the years,' Román assured her with a smile Laura saw was strained. The thought that he might be nervous

of meeting her parents occupied her thoughts
almost until they turned into the gates of the
Villa Castillo. Isabel darted down the steps from
the double front doors and enveloped Eleanor in
a voluminous embrace.

The emotional greeting between two old
friends passed largely over Laura's head as she
mounted the villa's wide-spaced steps. A cold
feeling of despair had closed over her with the
realisation that not even her father was immune
to Román's male charms. He had seemed
delighted by his future son-in-law's business
acumen on the drive back from the airport,
more than admiring as he followed the lithe
figure up the steps leading to the Villa Castillo.
She watched numbly her father's response to
the majestic hall with its central fountain
playing quietly on the lowest bowl where exotic
blossoms undulated gently with the movement
of the water.

'You certainly have a beautiful home here,'
John Benson remarked appreciatively, and Román
shrugged.

'The ancestor who built it was perhaps a little
ambitious,' he acknowledged, 'but I will be happy
to spend the rest of my life here.'

'And in the home you have near Mexico City,'
Isabel reminded him, laughing excitedly as she
turned to Eleanor. 'You must see his home in
Mexico, it is beyond description. Very modern
for my tastes, of course, but the subject of many
design magazine articles.'

Laura was surprised to hear this ... she had
imagined a confined, if luxurious, apartment in
the capital city, a nest to entertain his various

women friends. Now it seemed he preferred the greater privacy of a garden estate ... no doubt staffed by innumerable servants who took care of housekeeping and garden chores. It would all run smoothly, she was sure, when he entertained the latest love of his life. Her voice held a cool, taut quality as she invited her parents upstairs to the room adjoining her own.

'This is lovely,' her mother remarked brightly, investigating the tastefully furnished room and spacious attached bathroom.

John Benson agreed, but his eyes sobered as they focused on his daughter's guarded expression. 'He can certainly provide you with all the world's amenities,' he commented guardedly, 'and if this is what you want, kitten, then I'm happy.'

That would have been the moment to deny any real involvement with Román, but Laura had no time to do more than open her mouth before her mother emerged from the bathroom.

'It's all so beautiful,' she enthused fulsomely. 'I still can't believe you're going to marry this man, but I can understand why you'd want to. Apart from owning all this,' she waved a hand that encompassed the quarters she and her husband had been consigned, 'he's very attractive. Rather like an Arab sheik, with those dark eyes and pronounced brows.'

'If you two are going to discuss male attributes, I'm leaving,' grumbled John Benson, making good his threat by marching towards the door. 'Román said something about Mexican investments, which I'd like to pursue further—

you don't need me, honey, for the next little while?'

'Oh, go,' Eleanor waved him briskly away, turning to her daughter before the door finally closed on her husband's well-knit figure. 'Tell me all about it, darling, how it all happened. I mean, I can understand why you'd fall in love with such a man, but it all happened so quickly. Are you really in love with him?'

The question was one that any mother would have asked her daughter on the eve of her wedding, but Laura felt somehow that if she denied having fallen madly in love with Román her mother would be puzzled, disappointed with her daughter's weak-kneed agreement to marry Román.

'Yes, I—I guess I am,' she replied hesitantly, surprising herself with the surge of feeling that accompanied her words. Was it love when her heart tripped at the slightest touch of his hand, when every defensive measure she knew was readied to combat any objections her mother might fire at her?

'Good,' Eleanor rejoined briskly as she went to snap open the clasps of the suitcases Manuel had placed on racks at the foot of the canopied king-size bed. 'Then you won't mind hearing that Gavin Foster has plucked up the courage to divorce his wife, and that he'll be spending Christmas with the Stewarts at Lake Chapala, not far from here.' The Stewarts were British diplomats renowned for their sociability in foreign service circles, a couple Laura had met and vaguely liked in her travels with her parents. That they were sheltering for the holiday period the man she had once imagined herself in love with left Laura curiously cold.

'I'm glad Gavin has his freedom,' she remarked quietly, 'but I fell out of love with him a long time ago, Mother.'

'Yes, of course, darling,' her mother responded abstractedly, rummaging in one of the suitcases to extract finally a cerise-coloured long dress that she intended to wear that evening. 'Anyway, it's most unlikely we'll run into him while we're here.'

The casually spoken words couldn't have been more wrong. Later, when dinner was well through its preliminary stages, Laura heard Isabel proclaim delightedly, 'We must open up the house at Chapala for a week or so, and you will be able to meet with your friends. Don't you agree, Román?'

'Certainly, Tía,' he returned smoothly. 'I can spare only a day or two myself to enjoy the quiet beauty of the lake, but I am sure Laura and her parents will find it pleasurable.'

Another home! The extent of Castillo real estate holdings numbed the mind, Laura thought half resentfully, and she was allowing herself to slide into the untenable position of becoming yet another of Román's possessions. The farce had to end, and soon, but she could think of no way to do it without embarrassment to herself and deep humiliation for Román. A shiver ran lightly over her mostly bare shoulders when she recalled Román telling her about his ancestor, Don Román, who had punished his wife for her infidelities by incarcerating her in their bedroom for years . . . she had humiliated him, his pride had been hurt.

'You are deep in thought, *mi novia*,' said Román in a low voice intended only for herself, and she started and looked into the black eyes that searched her own, finding only the warm gleam of concern she was familiar with. But what had she expected? Today's Román lived in a far more civilised world than his temperamental ancestor.

'I—I was just wondering how many other homes you have that I haven't heard of yet,' she forced lightly, wondering if the smile that immediately lit up his face could possibly be of relief.

'No more, I promise you.' The smile faded and was replaced by a puzzled frown. 'Most women are ecstatic to find themselves the *châtelaine* of several houses, but you are not, *cara*, are you?'

His mention of other women, probably the ones who had thrown their marriage hopes into his ring, prompted her tart, 'Surely it's more important to love the man than his possessions,' and wished immediately she could have snatched the words back. His eyes filled with a fiery glitter as his hand covered hers and squeezed it.

'I believe you would still love me if I had nothing, *pequeña*,' he murmured emotionally, 'and that——'

'Now, you two,' Isabel interrupted in a loud voice from the other end of the table, her face flushed from the wine and the excitement, 'you are not married yet, so please remember there are other people in the world! Laura's father is

interested in buying a retirement property along
our sea coast, and I know nothing about that.'

Laura's head swivelled quickly to her father,
who was looking expectantly in Román's
direction, and then to her mother, who met her
gaze with a barely perceptible wink. Dear God,
things were becoming more deeply mired with
every minute that passed! Now her parents were
visualising a retirement life close, but not too
close, to the daughter who was to be married to a
Mexican and would naturally make her home
south of the border. She scarcely heard Román's
knowledgeable discourse on the advantages or
otherwise of various resort areas; she was only
conscious of his hand that still lay possessively
over hers, of the sickening certainty that she must
call a halt to the nightmare *now*, before the
original error was compounded beyond rescue.

But it wasn't until she was alone at last in her
room that a solution of sorts came to her. Gavin!
By a stroke of luck, he too would be at Lake
Chapala when the Castillo entourage moved
down there for a week. What more natural than
to find herself back in love with him, especially
now he was free? She wouldn't be, of course,
Gavin was a closed chapter in her life, one she
had no desire to re-open; but no one else would
know that, least of all Román. She would, of
course, take Gavin into her confidence . . . apart
from the dishonesty of it all, it would be
ridiculous to have two strings to a romantic bow
she had no wish to pluck.

The decision made, she dropped off to sleep
easily, but it was a sleep haunted by black eyes
that changed constantly from smouldering passion

to coolness to cruelty. The cruelty came last, and she felt Román's olive-skinned hands bind her tightly by the hands and feet, around the middle, until she could scarcely breathe. Even her vocal chords seemed to be pressured into silence.

Her eyes flew open when the overhead light was clicked on, and she stared dazedly at her mother as she advanced towards the bed in a pink floral robe and a waft of the perfume she had used for years.

'What is it, darling?' she asked softly, sitting on the bed beside Laura and lifting a hand to stroke the damp hair back from her heated forehead. 'Bad dream?'

'It wasn't a dream,' Laura whispered, her eyes darting wildly beyond her mother's head. 'Román . . . Román tied me up, he was so mad. . .'

'Nonsense, darling,' Eleanor returned mildly, easing off the bed to pull free the covers that had become wound tightly around her daughter's slender figure. 'You've been tossing and turning so much you've wrapped yourself up like a mummy—is that better?'

'But I—I couldn't even scream. . . .'

'You managed that much,' Eleanor retorted drily, 'or how would I have heard you? It was just a bad dream, darling. Too much excitement all at once.' She smiled and stroked again her daughter's tumbled hair. 'You and Román have fallen in love so quickly, it's bound to make you edgy thinking of all the ramifications, but it will work out, you'll see. One thing I know for sure— that man loves you as if he'd been waiting for you all his life. And you, my darling,' she pressed a gentle finger on the tip of Laura's nose as she got up, 'are just as crazy about him. I've never seen you with such a glow on as when you're with Román. I'm happy for you,' she ended simply, giving Laura a misty smile. 'Now I must get back before your father wonders where I am. Goodnight, my precious.'

Laura lay in the dark long after her mother had switched off the light and left the room, leaving the echoes of her softly spoken words. She had no doubts about the rightness of the marriage she expected would take place; even in such a short time she had made her judgement about Román's feelings towards her daughter, hers towards him. But she was wrong, wrong. . .

The night before the family exodus to Lake Chapala, Laura came down early to dinner and wandered out to the covered terrace where *merienda* had been served that afternoon. All traces of the afternoon snack had been cleared away by unobtrusive servants, and the terrace now looked like a stage set just before the curtain rose on the first act.

Laura moved restlessly into the open garden area and sat on the wrought iron bench under the flame tree. All day, during the tour Román had given her parents and herself of his offices and the late lunch at his club afterwards, her mother's words had continued to haunt her. 'I've never seen you with such a glow on as when you're with Román.' Perhaps in the beginning she had fancied herself a little in love with him—what woman wouldn't, given his looks, his wealth, his unassailable confidence? In her case, there had been the additional attraction of his likeness to the main character in her new novel. Although she had set out to destroy Felipe Alvarez and all he arrogantly stood for, there had been something about his character that appealed to all that was female in her. But Román? For the first time she seemed to see him clearly. He was no Felipe Alvarez, nor yet a character replica of his cruel ancestor, Don Román. Had he been, Nicolas would have been tossed out on his ear to sink or swim years ago, but Román still kept up the pretence that the younger man was pulling his weight in the family business, even after the fiasco of the Garcia contract, which Nicolas had evidently mismanaged.

The fountain had been left on this evening, and that was perhaps why she was unaware of another presence in the garden, until arms went round her from behind and a hand came up to turn her face to a warm, eager kiss that went on and on until she felt the trapped breath in her throat begin to choke her.

'Forgive me if I startled you,' Román murmured hotly at her ear finally, his own breath sounding laboured, 'but you looked so beautiful here in the garden all by yourself, I couldn't resist. And you must admit, *cara*,' he teased, leaving her momentarily to come round and sit close to her, 'that I have had very few crumbs to spread on my table of love these past few days. It is as if you feel your parents will not understand the need we have to be alone together, yet they are still in love themselves after so many years.'

Laura drew a quivering breath. It was true she had made her parents the excuse for retiring when they did each evening; she hadn't wanted to deepen Román's misunderstanding of her feelings. Now, suddenly, she didn't know herself what her feelings were. She was confused, and Román's close proximity wasn't making matters any less so. She was too aware of his physical presence, the firm pressure of his shoulder against hers, the taut thigh that set up an inexplicable trembling in hers, the shadows that came and went on his face with the movement of the flame tree above them. She had all the symptoms of love without feeling its reality.

'Román, I—I have to talk to you,' she began hesitantly, knowing that honesty was, after all, the best policy.

'Talk? There is plenty of time for that later,' he brushed her words aside and put his arms around her, drawing her to him. His voice came muzzled from where he pressed his lips to her neck. 'Now we must make the most of these few moments together . . . ah, Laura, if only you could know all that is in my heart, but I am a poor spokesman in this matter.'

Laura would have disagreed had she possessed the breath to do so, but as his voice went brokenly on she found herself responding almost against her will to the sheer physical magnetism of him. Her body seemed to have a separate will of its own, pressing hungrily to Román's as he tilted her head to the angle of his lips and kissed her with a wildness that made her forget she had been about to tell him she didn't love him. She made no objection to rising at his touch to stand with him under the sheltering flame tree branches and press the eager warmth of her body to the downcurve of his, mindless except for the

violent need to merge herself with him, become
one with him. Her breast quivered in response to
the hand he slid under the low neck of her dress,
the nipple hardening under the unfamiliar caress
of his fingers.

The murmur of voices from the hall penetrated
only slightly, but when Isabel called, 'Román?
Laura? Are you out there?' Laura pulled away
with a gasp.

'Relax,' Román said lightly, seeming amused
by her stiff withdrawal. 'They all know what it is
to be in love and to want to be alone together.'
He slid an arm around her waist and drew her
back to him for a featherlight kiss on her half-
opened lips. 'Just twelve more days to our
marriage,' he murmured, 'and then we can tell
them all to go to the devil.'

Laura wasn't at all sure she wanted to tell her
mother, who was smiling her approval at her
daughter's flushed cheeks, or her father, who
stood with Nicolas in the background looking
happy yet somehow sad at the same time, to go to
the devil. A completely new warmth towards
humankind filled her, even when Isabel said
tartly before leading the way back into the house.

'Your cook will be furious, Román, if we keep
her meal waiting.'

'Then she will just have to take her spite out on
her pots and pans,' he retorted mildly, 'or make
her living elsewhere.'

It was only when she was seated in her usual
place beside his right hand that Laura knew she
was in love with him. Every syllable he uttered in
his huskily attractive voice, every expressive
movement of his olive-skinned hands, had a

sensual significance for her. Her thoughts leapt ahead to when she, and not Isabel, would take her place at the other end of the long dining table, when dark-eyed sons and pretty daughters would replace the diners of tonight. An overwhelming sense of relief brought a brilliance to her smile whenever Román glanced her way. There was no need now to enlist Gavin's services as a would-be lover . . . she had the only lover she would ever want right here beside her.

Shadows and sunlight played on the hills surrounding Lake Chapala as they drove south from Guadalajara, and Laura's breath drew in along with the others when they caught their first glimpse of the lake that seemed more like a sea in its infinity. Islands dotting its misty blue surface added to the impression.

'I'm afraid the lake will be too cold to swim in,' Isabel informed the rest of the passengers, 'but the Villa Vista has its own heated pool. Your friends will be welcome to come and swim there,' she said graciously to Eleanor, who accepted happily although, she said aloud, she wasn't sure that the villa her friends had rented was without a pool. 'I can't imagine that Margot Stewart would take a place without one, can you, darling?' she directed to Laura. 'Margot once made a stab at the Olympics,' she turned to explain to Isabel, 'and she's never forgotten it since.'

The Villa Vista was all that Laura had expected and more. High walls surrounded the entrance courtyard where bougainvillea, in a brilliant purple shade, spilled over and softened the fortress-like appearance. Immense wooden gates, fulsomely carved, opened to admit the car to a courtyard that was partly given over to garden squares and triangles where brilliantly coloured flowers vied for attention, but mostly it was paved and served as an entrance to the house itself. A jumbled pile of flaking white plaster, it looked as if it had grown there by its own whimsy; basically a two-storey structure, wings and towers had obviously been added haphazardly with no thought of overall unity of design. Still, there was something comfortably attractive about it, an impression that deepened when Laura walked with the others into a central hall that opened directly on to a large living room with a window wall overlooking lawned gardens and the lake beyond. Far from the antique air of the Villa Castillo, this house exuded relaxation in its deeply padded sofas and chairs upholstered in bright, cheerful florals. Isabel evidently didn't agree with her.

'So many times I have offered to refurbish this house,' she lamented, 'but Román likes it the way it is. Perhaps you will be able to influence him, Laura, when you are married,' she directed a long-suffering look in Laura's direction.

'I wouldn't dream of it,' she said happily, walking over to take in the peaceful view, 'because I like it just the way it is, too. It's just what a resort home should be ... comfortable and relaxing, and you don't have to worry about sand in the rugs or heelmarks on the coffee table.'

'Ah, you are well suited, you two,' Isabel gave up in disgust, not knowing how much her words had thrilled Laura as she busied herself directing the guests to their rooms on the upper floor. Laura, however, hugged them to her as she followed the others up a scarred wood central staircase that branched off to left and right when it reached the second storey hallway.

Well suited! Was it possible that two people from such divergent backgrounds could be compatible in the close ties of marriage? A few days ago she would have emphatically denied such a possibility, but now only the tremulous excitement of her suddenly discovered love held sway. Within it, everything seemed possible. Román was a product of the twentieth century, not the eighteenth, when wives secluded themselves in their marital homes and thought about nothing more serious than which dress to wear for this or that function. She would carry on with her writing and carve her own niche in the world, and Román would be proud of her.

The room she had been given was large and square apart from the sloping ceilings surrounding the latticed windows overlooking the rear gardens and lake. From here she glimpsed the azure blue of the swimming pool Isabel had mentioned, and promised herself a dip before too much time went by. She turned as her mother came into the room.

'The place may look archaic,' she said with an air of surprise, 'but it seems to have been brought up to date in the past thirty years or so. We have our own bathroom, though I'm not too sure about the tub—it's so deep I'll surprise myself if I can get out of it once in. How about you?'

Laura shrugged. 'I haven't checked on things like that yet, but have you seen the view? It makes me wish I could paint, with those hazy blue hills in the background.'

'You must be in love,' her mother retorted crisply. 'As an infant, you weren't remotely interested in finger painting at kindergarten.'

'I really think I am—in love, I mean.' Laura turned dreamily back to the view. 'Is it possible to fall this much in love that quickly?'

'Well, your father and I decided half an hour after meeting that we wanted to spend our lives together, so yes, I'd say it's possible. There's just one difference, darling,' Eleanor hesitated.

'And that is?' Laura turned back to face her mother, her blue eyes filled with question.

'Well, I—To put it bluntly, darling, are you sure you're not overwhelmed by all this?' Eleanor waved an encompassing hand towards the room, but Laura knew she was indicating the larger world of Román Castillo and all that entailed. 'Don't misunderstand me, I think Román is every woman's dream, but—is he yours, Laura?'

A flash of irritation made Laura turn away and walk towards the double bed covered by a colourful, homespun bedspread. Eleanor was being as fluctuating in her thoughts as ever; on the night of her dream of being tied up by a vengeful Román, her mother had told her how happy she was for her. Now it seemed she was having second thoughts. Laura smoothed one hand over the thick tapestry design of the bedcover, feeling the close hand-weaving of the raised flowers.

'Yes, he's my dream, Mother,' she said in a controlled voice. 'I—wasn't sure to begin with, but now I am. And I wouldn't care if he had nothing, if he made his living begging at street corners,' she added passionately, knowing it was true.

Her father's voice came plaintively from the door. 'Aren't we supposed to go down for lunch? Something smells real good.'

'Oh, John, nothing ever puts you off your food, does it?' Eleanor crossed to the door and ruffled his thinning hair affectionately.

'Not when all I have for breakfast is a couple of rolls and a dab of jelly,' he retorted drily, turning his head to look at Laura as he slid an arm around Eleanor's waist to propel her through the doorway, 'Coming, kitten?'

'In a minute, Dad.'

She stood deep in thought after her parents went out, a frown curving down between her brows. Could she really be as in love as she had thought if a few well chosen words from her mother had the effect of making her doubt her relationship with Román? If only he had been able to come down to Lake Chapala with them! Feeling his arms around her, his mouth eager on hers, would consign those doubts to where they belonged, she knew. But business had to come first . . . business always would, with Román. . .

CHAPTER EIGHT

'ELEANOR, I just couldn't wait for you to come and visit us, especially when I discovered you were just down the road from our villa!'

The midday meal was almost over when Margot Stewart, a tall rawboned woman in her late forties, her sandy-coloured hair too springily thick to be controlled by style, strode into the room ignoring the protests of the houseman, Enrique, who together with his wife, Matilda, took care of the villa year round. Laura thought wryly that the poor man had probably never encountered such a breezily confident woman as Margot before. It was a confidence bred from an aristocratic background in England reinforced by her husband's prominent position in the diplomatic service, not to mention her own prowess in sports.

Eleanor rose, hastily dabbing her mouth and throwing the napkin down on the table before turning to greet the friend she had shared many foreign outposts with.

'Margot, how lovely to see you! It's been what, two years?' After an exchange of hugs, she turned to the company and introduced the brown-eyed Margot. Isabel was coolly polite, reflecting the shock she had felt at the Englishwoman's forced entry into the villa.

John Benson rose from his place to shake hands and bestow a kiss on Margot's cheek, asking about her husband, Howard.

'Oh, he and Gavin have taken a busman's holiday,' she returned airily, 'and are spending the day with the American Consul in Guadalajara. You remember Gavin Foster, don't you, Laura?' Perhaps Laura was being over-sensitive, but she could have sworn there was a malicious glint in the hard brown eyes. 'You and he were quite a thing at one time, weren't you, but there was always his wife and children. Anyway, you probably know by now that he's free as a bird— Vanessa divorced him in the end. She was totally unsuited as a Service wife anyway, never wanted to be parted from the children. Whereas with your background, my dear, you know before you start that there won't be any stable home for your children, if you should have any.'

She ran out of breath and there was an embarrassed pause, so that she looked enquiringly at Eleanor.

'I'm afraid Gavin no longer features in Laura's life,' she said quietly. 'She's marrying Román Castillo, the man who owns this villa, in a matter of days.'

Margot's jaw dropped. 'But Gavin thinks——!' She turned accusing eyes on Laura. 'Why haven't you let him know that you're marrying this Mexican, whoever he is? He'll be devastated to hear this!'

Before Laura had time to retort that she and Gavin had not been in touch for many months, and it was none of Margot's business anyway, Eleanor stepped in adroitly.

'Señora Castillo here is Román's aunt, and my very good friend since our Mexico days.' The warning went over Margot's head and Isabel, who sat with snapping eyes at the head of the table, was far from mollified, though her innate courtesy would not permit her to be rude to a guest, even an uninvited one.

'Please be seated, *señora*,' she invited with restrained dignity, 'and join us for coffee.'

Margot had not spent years as a diplomat's wife without learning something about tact. An awkward colour reddening her freckled cheeks, she took the proffered chair and murmured, '*Gracias, señora.* I hope you will forgive my bursting in like this, but I was anxious to see Eleanor and her family.'

Isabel bent her head in haughty acknowledgement, but she was obviously relieved when the party broke up some fifteen minutes later, John and Eleanor accepting Margot's invitation to inspect her rented villa, Laura having made the excuse that she had work to do on her book, Isabel drew her aside as everyone moved out of the dining room.

'She is not—*simpatica*, that woman,' she tossed her head at Margot's departing back, then turned her flashing eyes on Laura's. 'This—Gabeen she speaks of, he is the married man you told me of?'

Laura frowned, then her brow cleared. 'Oh, *Gavin!* Yes, he is the one,' she answered honestly. 'But that was over long ago, Tia Isabel, and he never meant as much to me as Román does now.' She had used the word 'aunt' for the first time in addressing Isabel, and a warm glow tinged her cheeks with pink. Somehow it made her feel closer to Román, and miss him a little less.

'Take care, *niña*, that Román understands this

also. He would be—*formidable* if he suspects that
you are meeting this man who once meant much
to you.'

'Román trusts me, I hope.' Laura walked on to
the foot of the stairs, betraying her irritation
though she knew that Isabel had given the advice
with the best of intentions. She turned back
sharply, one foot on the bottom step, when Isabel
spoke again.

'Perhaps it is this man he would not trust,' she
said softly. 'My nephew is a proud man and likes
to keep what is his. Why do you think he keeps
Nicolas so busy in his office?'

Laura stared blankly. 'Nicolas?'

The older woman smiled half proudly. 'Nico is
very attractive to women, Román knows this.
Even Mercedes was taken with him the night she
came to dinner, and I suspect she has seen him
since.'

Reverting to formality, Laura said coolly, 'I
think you are mistaken, *señora*. Now if you'll
excuse me, I would like to do some work.'

But she made no attempt to unpack the
typewriter and manuscript notes she had brought
with her, standing instead looking with little
interest at the view spread before her. *Was*
Román as possessive as his aunt had indicated?
He had shown no signs of it, even when Eleanor
had announced that Gavin would be—but no, she
hadn't mentioned Gavin in front of Román, only
that the Stewarts would be at Lake Chapala. It
really wasn't important . . . wasn't that what love
meant, trusting each other? She herself hadn't
given one thought to the women Román might be
seeing in Guadalajara this week; the opportunity

would be there, but the desire for other company missing, as it was for her. As for Nicolas——

A frown ruffled the smoothness of her brow. It was true she hadn't seen much of him lately, even at dinner, but that was surely because he had been badly scared by the mess he had made of the Garcia contract, enough to stir himself up to prove to Román that he was worthy of a place in the family business.

The lake was a cool grey-blue now, matching the pensive quality of her mood. For the first time, she wondered if being in love was enough. Marriage in general required a large amount of give and take ... and marriage between two people so far apart in background, experience and even language took on an added burden. Was the love she was so sure about now sufficient to carry them through the inevitable trials and tribulations that lay ahead? Her mind going off on a tangent, she wondered what her reaction would be on meeting Gavin Foster again. She had thought herself in love with him, too, but that had been so different from what she now felt for Román; probably the fact of his being married had added a touch of illicit spice, drama to the situation.

Annoyed by her own introspection, she squared her shoulders and went to unpack her writing materials.

Her question about how she would react to meeting Gavin again was resolved the next afternoon when she went down to the villa's pool, a haphazardly shaped blue-green outline that boasted a small island at its centre covered with small fan palms and the brilliant red of poinsettias, lending an exotic air to the sweeping lawns of lush green surrounding the pool.

Despite the sun shining from a clear blue sky, the water was warmer than the surrounding air, and she plunged happily into it in the light gold of her bikini. Her parents were spending the day with the Stewarts, investigating the boutiques of the nearby village of Ajijic which were famous for their handwoven cloth goods and quality gift items. Laura had declined their invitation to go with them, admitting now as she swam in leisurely fashion around the nooks and crannies of the pool that her real excuse had been that she hadn't wanted to see it all for the first time in Gavin's company. Román would take her at the weekend when he came down from the city, and it would be another lovely day like the one in Tlaquepaque when they had wandered hand in hand.

'Laura?'

Startled when the familiar voice addressed her, she sank below the glittering surface of the pool and let water into her nose and mouth. Spluttering, she came up two or three yards from where immaculately creased off-white trousers and expensive leather sandals stood at the edge. Her eyes lifted as she trod water to the navy casual shirt that lent depth to Gavin's pale blue eyes set in a light-skinned face that contrasted sharply with the deep brown of his, she noticed, thinning hair.

'Gavin,' she gulped on the chlorinated water at the back of her throat, 'how nice to see you.'

'I was strolling along the beach and happened to see you,' he said in his medium-pitched voice that she remembered so well. 'No, that's a lie,' he added, startling her again, but this time she managed to keep her head above water. 'I came along this way in the hopes of seeing you, since you weren't joining the others in their shopping spree. I have to speak to you, Laura,' he added almost desperately.

'Do you mind if I get out of here first?' Laura strove for a flippancy that didn't quite come off. A sinking feeling in her middle told her that she was in for a sticky interview with the man who had once meant so much to her, but now seemed impossibly serious with his exaggerated stoop and long, solemn features.

She paddled to the side and pulled herself up to a sitting and then a standing position, gaining time to assimilate her reaction to him by squeezing the moisture from her hair in a sideways motion. 'I'll get my wrap,' she murmured, padding over to the chair where she had left it and draping it round her shoulders, uncomfortably aware of his encompassing stare over the scanty lines of her bikini.

'Well, you look very well, Gavin,' she said in a politely restrained voice, relieved when his gaze lifted to her face.

'And you look more beautiful than ever,' he returned with a hoarseness that embarrassed her. 'Now that I'm with you again, I can't believe I've let three years go by without seeing you. God, Laura, you can't know how much I've wanted to!'

'Until recently you've known where to find me,' she pointed out with a touch of wryness which she immediately regretted because it sounded like a reproach. 'Let's sit down—can I get you something to drink?' His quick frown indicated that he had noted her studied change to polite sociability.

'You already act like the lady of the house,' his voice held a faint sneer, 'Señora Castillo, I believe it's to be?'

Laura narrowed her eyes against the sun as she looked up at him. 'Yes,' she said shortly.

'You can't seriously see yourself as the wife of that Spanish *grandee*, can you?'

'I wouldn't be marrying him next week if I couldn't see myself as his wife,' she retorted tartly. 'I don't think your opinion of him is valid, either, since you've never met him——'

'Ah, but I have,' he cut in, surprising her. 'Yesterday, in fact, when we went to lunch with the American Embassy people. He was having lunch at the same place—in the company, I might add, of a ravishingly beautiful woman.'

Laura would have liked to show no reaction to his taunting, but the sharp stab of jealous uncertainty that twisted in her stomach made her feel sick, and she knew that her cheeks had paled under the light gold tan she had acquired. She stared in numbed pain at Gavin, who dropped into the chair adjoining hers, his attitude of snide aloofness crumbling as he leaned forward earnestly, one hand touching and curling round her forearm.

'That was a rotten thing to say, Laura, and I'm sorry. The blonde was probably some business acquaintance or out-of-town relative he had to entertain.'

The blonde! For a moment Laura had had the

idea that the woman might have been Mercedes, back in Guadalajara for some reason, but the hope died painfully ... by no stretch of the imagination could Mercedes be described as a blonde! She licked her lips, which had suddenly dried as if they were about to crack.

'He—um—does a lot of business entertaining,' she said weakly, and knew that Gavin wasn't fooled for an instant.

'How could you have agreed to marry a man like that?' he burst out. 'You know what Latins are like, that this kind of thing will go on after as well as before, it's an accepted way of life for them, loyalty doesn't enter into it.' He had the grace to flush when Laura's head whipped round to give him a scathing look. 'I know what you're thinking, that I wasn't all that loyal to Vanessa, but that was different. She refused to live with me as my wife unless I did what she wanted and give up my career for a boring office job in London. I—realised when we parted that I hadn't been fair to you either. That's why I was determined not to see you until the divorce was final, which happened only a month ago.'

Laura said nothing, and he went on in a lowered tone, 'I still love you, Laura, and want you to marry me. That's why it was such a shock to find that you're engaged to this—this Castillo fellow. I couldn't believe it.'

'Did you really expect me to hang on the tree like an overripe plum until you decided to come along and pick me eventually?' Laura stirred from her lethargy to toss out angrily, then waved a dismissive hand. 'Not that it occurred to me to wait for you, we made no such agreement. And incidentally, wasn't it Vanessa who divorced you, not the other way round?'

Gavin flushed again and removed his hand from her arm, straightening. 'I did the gentlemanly thing, of course,' he said stiffly.

'Oh, for heaven's sake, Gavin, don't be so stuffy! As if anyone cares about the "gentlemanly thing" these days!' Laura jumped to her feet, knowing she was venting her bitterness over Román's perfidy rather than condemning Gavin for a quality she had once admired in him. 'Look, I'm sorry,' she apologised shortly, 'I guess I was upset over what you said about Román and—this woman. But the truth of it is that I trust him and he trusts me, so I know there's a perfectly good reason for them to have been together.' God, was she trying to convince him or herself? Before she had time to decide, Gavin leapt to his feet and made a lunge for her, his long arms pinning hers to her body as he drew her up to him.

'Have you gone mad?' she gasped, struggling vainly to free herself. 'Let me go this instant, Gavin, damn you!'

'Not until we've put your Latin lover's trust to the test,' he gritted through clenched teeth, his eyes narrowing to a blue-grey glint.

'W-what?'

For answer his head bent and his mouth came down hard on hers, crushing her lips painfully against her teeth so that her senses swam. The scent of his skin, of the aftershave lotion he used, was strong in her nostrils, making her stomach churn. He had to be mad! The divorce, then finding her about to marry someone else, had preyed on his mind . . . sheer fright gave strength to her struggles, and finally he released one arm, which rose and then fell on to his shoulder, pushing, grinding at the smooth cotton of his navy shirt.

He released her as quickly as he had grabbed her, his breath only slightly heavier as he smiled without mirth and nodded towards the house. 'I think the trust between you two is mutually weak.'

Laura's head whipped sideways and she stiffened with shock to see Román standing stockstill at the top of the grassy rise that sloped up from the pool. For a moment she couldn't believe she was seeing the face of the man who had changed the whole direction of her life with his love. She had seen it in so many expressions, eyes glinting with humour or passion, mouth relaxed, smiling, and on occasion his brows knitted in a frown. Now all those features seemed frozen into granite hardness, his eyes even at a distance shrivelling her with the cold contempt in them. She felt her knees were about to buckle and she sagged against Gavin for a moment, hardly realising that she did so, but when Román spun on his heel and strode rapidly towards the house, she started forward crying desperately, 'Román! Román, wait!'

Irritably she struck at Gavin, who had followed her and grabbed her arm. 'Haven't you done enough damage?' she demanded savagely. 'What is it with you, anyway? Do you just hate to see anybody else happy when you're not?'

'Believe it or not,' he dodged her flailing fist, 'it's your happiness I'm thinking of.' He succeeded in capturing her free arm, and gave her a light shake. 'I had to prove to you that you'd be doing the wrong thing in marrying Castillo. It just wouldn't work, Laura.'

'Since when have you become the expert on what works in marriage?' she panted scathingly, and he let her go immediately, his face taking on a remote dignity.

'Perhaps it's because I know from experience what won't work,' he said quietly, making Laura pause in her flight after Román. 'My marriage didn't because Vanessa's and my interests were miles apart. The same thing can happen to you if you marry this man.'

'I'll take the chance,' she threw at him before breaking into a run, her breath coming in snatches as she rushed into the hall and saw that it was empty apart from the ageing Enrique, who lifted his brows in surprise at her haste.

'Señor Castillo?' she gasped, and he shrugged bewilderedly.

'He was here, señorita, but now,' he looked at the wide open hall door, 'he has gone again.'

'Did he—say when he will come back?'

The old servant lifted his shoulders in another significant shrug. 'He said nothing, señorita, but I have known him from a child and saw that he was very angry about something. It happens not often with him but when he is like that we walk softly around him.' If the elderly man suspected that Laura was responsible for his master's black mood, he tactfully gave no indication of it. He nodded and smiled when she thanked him, then made his way to the side door that led to the kitchen quarters, leaving Laura standing biting her lip in the middle of the hall.

She had to talk to him, explain—would he believe the truth when she told him? Her mind was still dazed from what had happened, but even to her it seemed like a wildly impossible excuse, made up on the spur of the moment. Damn Gavin and his misguided intentions! She swivelled uncertainly on her heel, then went to the stairs and ran decisively up them. If Román hadn't come back in a couple of hours—if he wasn't just driving around the area to cool his temper—she would beg, borrow or steal a car and pursue him to Guadalajara. Seeing him face to face, though she quailed inwardly at the thought of confronting his anger, would be much better than using the telephone. He could cut her off on that without hearing her explanation, but he would be forced to hear her out at the Villa Castillo.

Dusk was already shrouding the mountains and creeping over the fields as Laura drove along the road filled with unexpectedly deep potholes, but the comfortably sprung family-sized car barely noted them before carrying smoothly on to Guadalajara.

She had been amazed at the ease with which she had made her departure from the Villa Vista. It had been simplicity itself to send a message downstairs saying that she wanted to work on for a while, she would eat later. No one came to dissuade her, presuming, she supposed, that they accepted her need to carry on while the muse was on her. Isabel and her parents had been safely closeted in the dining room when she crept downstairs; her only concern now was to find a

vehicle she could drive, and with luck with the
keys left in it. Otherwise, she would have to find
Manuel and explain that she wanted to drive
herself into the city.

As it happened, it was Enrique who discovered
her tiptoeing across the hall, his brows rising in
surprise when he saw her dressed for outdoors, a
warm waist-length jacket over her thin wool
dress.

'You are going out, *señorita*?' he asked. 'Señora
Castillo told me you did not want to be disturbed
to eat. . .'

Laura had decided to take the elderly man into
her confidence—she could hardly have done
anything else, she reflected now wryly, swerving
the wheel and barely missing the biggest void so
far on the journey. It had taken quite a lot of
persuasion to convince him that she had to see
Román immediately, and that no, she didn't need
Manuel to drive her. After a lot of headshaking
and misgivings, Enrique had joined in her
conspiracy and brought the keys to what he felt
was the safest car, still muttering as he opened
the huge wooden doors to permit her exit.

She glanced at the illuminated dial clock. Soon
now Enrique would explain to her parents and
Isabel that she had had to see Román urgently
. . . they wouldn't be surprised at that, what
bride-to-be didn't feel the need to be with her
loved one at this stage in their marriage plans?

If only that were the only reason she had for
braving this constantly darkening country road,
where the occasional carcase of a cow or even a
horse at its verge bore mute evidence of the
danger of driving after dark. Román had not

returned, so obviously he had believed the evidence of his eyes. How could he do that? Laura raged inwardly for the umpteenth time. He must know she loved him, that she would never have agreed to marry him for any other reason. He was probably thinking right now that she was marrying him for the same reasons all those other women had laid their nets for him . . . for his name, his wealth, his prestige.

She hadn't given a thought to the build-up of traffic in the evening rush hour, and all thoughts of everything else slid into the background as she manoeuvred the awkwardly large car around one traffic circle after another, breathing a sigh of relief when she found herself on the Avenue Chapultepec with its graceful, brightly illuminated fountains down its centre. She knew her way from there.

The Villa Castillo seemed unlit except for the protective exterior lamps lighting strategic points, and her heart sank. What if Román hadn't come back here after all? The servants had probably been given at least the night off since the family was away at the lake. It surprised her to find the parking gates wide open, a car parked at an off angle to the service door. Román's car! So he had come back here—she wasn't sure if she was glad or sorry. The words she had rehearsed for two hours in her room at the Villa Vista deserted her. He wouldn't have believed them anyway. Perhaps he had wiped her out of his life already, maybe the blonde woman he had lunched with yesterday was here with him now.

The hall was only dimly lit, and no lights shone from Román's quarters—but then they wouldn't be visible behind the thickly panelled doors. Laura turned to the small carved table inside the rear entrance door to lay her handbag on it, not noticing the porcelain figurine the bag's corner caught until it was teetering dangerously on the bevelled edge. She made a lunge for it, but it slipped from her erratic grasp and crashed to the floor, shattering into a hundred pieces. The noise of its contact with the marble floor was tremendous, and she stared frozenly up at the underpart of the right-curving stairway. Only seconds passed, although it seemed a century to her, until a door was thrown open above and a shaft of light fell on to the floor inches away.

'Who's that?' Román's voice demanded, strangely thick-sounding.

'It—it's me, Laura.' Her legs seemed frozen to the spot, but she finally made them move until she was standing in the light thrown down from Román's living room. 'I didn't mean to startle you, but it's so dark in here. I'm so sorry about the——'

'Dark?' he interrupted brusquely, his shadowy figure moving further back into the upper hall, and seconds later the lower one was filled with such bright lights that Laura blinked. 'That's better, isn't it?' He advanced to the head of the stairs and looked down at her stonily. He was still dressed in the cream shirt and beige trousers of the afternoon, but his hair looked as if fifty hands had ploughed their way through it.

'Román, I——'

'How did you get here?' he interrupted harshly, starting down the stairs without touching the banister.

'I—d-drove,' she said hesitantly.

'Where is Manuel?'

'Back at Lake Chapala. He didn't know I was coming here.' She had no intention of getting the servants into trouble for her sake. 'I—took the car without him knowing.'

'Hah! In the same way you thought to steal much of what I possess by marrying me?' He had reached her now, and Laura realised with a sense of shock that he had been drinking heavily. Apart from the strong odour of whisky on his breath, his pupils were mere pinpoints in his mocking eyes. 'Did your lover send you here to make up with me, *cara*, so that he will not lose his share in the—what do you call it?—alimony settlement when eventually we divorce?'

Laura drew in a sharp breath. 'Gavin is not my lover in the sense you mean,' she denied levelly, 'and as for the rest, it's nonsense. I've never been motivated by money, yours or anyone else's, nor has Gavin as far as I know. What you saw this afternoon was planned by him deliberately to—to break us up, you and I. He—thinks it would be a mistake for us to marry because of the difference in our backgrounds.'

'Very altruistic of him,' Román managed to put a sneer into his seemingly agreeable nod. 'And I suppose he would rescue you himself, if he did not already have a wife.'

Laura's gaze fell from his and she stared at the vee of black hair revealed by the loosened top buttons of his shirt. 'He—no longer has a wife,' she said weakly. 'His divorce came through a month ago.'

'Ah, the plot thickens,' Román mocked lightly,

as if what was happening amused him, nothing more. 'Until this afternoon, everything was going to plan, but then I had to spoil it all for you, didn't I?' He made no move towards her, yet Laura felt suddenly menaced by the hard glitter in his narrowed eyes. 'You were not expecting me at the Villa Vista this afternoon, so I interrupted the plot you had hatched between you. You would engage my affections—which you did, I must admit—while your lover set the wheels in motion for his divorce. A brief, but you would hope sweet marriage to me, and then yet another divorce which would free you and the money I would settle on you in order to rid myself of you, and the end of all fairy tales—you and he would live happily together.'

Laura's eyes were wide blue orbs acknowledging his ingenuous, if totally inaccurate, summation of the situation. 'I was right in suggesting that you'd be a better writer of fiction than I,' she said acidly, staring him out with renewed courage. 'But fiction is just what it implies—it's untrue. Gavin has meant nothing to me——'

'Now do you understand my ancestor, Don Román, and his desire to punish the wife who was unfaithful to him?' Román interrupted savagely, ignoring her protestation. His hand made a sudden swift movement and dragged her hair from its confining pins as it raked through and fastened on its lower thickness. Laura found herself staring into the eyes of the madman he had become, his strong lean fingers pulling painfully on the roots of her hair. A nightmare situation had suddenly become one fraught with physical danger.

'Román, please don't do this ... you don't understand!'

'I understand perfectly, my dear,' he jerked her head back and up so that she was forced to look at him. 'Do you remember that I told you Castillo men cannot bear humiliation at the hands of their women? Don Román had his own way of subduing the woman who had sworn to love him ... I have mine!'

Without warning Laura found herself being dragged across the hall to the staircase opposite his own, Román's fingers pulling painfully at her hair. Humiliation mingled with a childish desire to cry from the pain accompanied each step on the way up to the higher level, where he veered off in the direction of the room she had investigated her first morning in the Villa. Disregarding the agonising tugs at her scalp, Laura began to twist desperately to free herself. This was the room where Don Román had imprisoned his errant wife for umpteen years, making sure she saw no other male but him to assuage her capricious appetites! Román obviously intended to punish her in similar fashion, for what he regarded as similar transgressions, and the injustice of it lent strength to her struggles, though she might have been made of pliable straw for all the effect she made on the grimly determined Román. She felt herself thrown into the middle of the room, free at last from the binding hold on her hair but completely disorientated in the darkness. Hysteria threatened to bubble out in nameless pleadings, and then the lights were switched on with dazzling brightness so that she blinked as she stared up into Román's hawklike remoteness.

'So now we will discover,' he said with harsh dryness, 'just which of us you prefer as a lover!'

CHAPTER NINE

Aching in every part of her body, Laura lay staring at the dust-laden canopy sheltering the bed that had been unused for a century or more . . . until last night. Had Don Román's wife awakened each morning as deadened in her senses as Laura now did? Her husband, extracting vengeance, had no doubt taken her as impersonally as Román had taken Laura last night, but at least the woman in that case had been used to the physical desires of men, as Laura was not.

Like the thawing of winter-long ice, shivers started deep in her abdomen and spread as far as the fingertips clutching the bedspread that had been carelessly tossed over her nakedness. With true arrogance, Román had used her and discarded her. Her mind shrank from the memory of being roughly parted from her clothes and tossed backwards like a doll on the bed that exuded dust at every movement, of being forcefully stripped of dignity in the most intimate parts of her being, mind and body.

What did it matter now, she thought dully, that Román had seemed sobered, even shocked, when at last he pushed himself away from the bed and drew on the clothes he had savagely discarded? Without his trust, the night that should have been filled with the joy of their first coming together had been a mockery of one superior physical force dominating another. There had been nothing of love in the taking or giving, in this room imbued with a sadness she now understood. Giving gladly was one thing; being forced was something else entirely.

She was dressed in the clothes she picked up from the floor where they had been strewn when a single tap sounded at the door and it was pushed decisively open. Román's appearance shocked her, although she had been sure that nothing could ever accomplish that again. Her own eyes reflected in the faded mirror over the dresser had shown her that there were smudges under them, but Roman's looked positively bruised against the sickly pallor of his facial skin. It was obvious he had slept even less than she, probably not at all.

'I have come to apologise,' he said stiffly, his voice bearing traces of hangover thickness, 'and to tell you that our marriage will take place as planned.'

Laura stifled an insane desire to laugh hysterically. What absolute arrogance to think she would dream of linking her life with a man who felt obliged to marry her because he had violated the virginity he had thought she no longer possessed!

'Oh no, Don Román,' she stressed the title coolly, and saw by the tightening of his jaw that he understood the reference to his despotic forebear, 'the marriage will not take place, as planned or ever.'

'What?' He seemed genuinely startled, as if he had expected her undying gratitude for his willingness to face up to his responsibility.

Laura bent to pick up the one remaining item

of hers on the floor, her handbag, and searched
with abstract coolness for her tube of lipstick and
comb. Her fingers occupied themselves with the
familiar routine of touching colour to her lips and
straightening the tangled skeins of her hair. The
red-gold strands gleamed dully back to her from
the faded mirror, like a wedding ring dimmed by
time.

Holding her voice steady, she said brittlely,
'I've never really cared much if the man I
eventually married was rich or poor, handsome or
ugly, as long as I could respect him. After last
night, that's impossible with you. I'm leaving
Mexico as soon as my parents and I can collect
my things.'

Román started forward until she could see his
ravaged expression in the mirror, then he halted
abruptly and stared tightlipped at her profile. 'I
have offered you my apology for an act I regret
very much,' he said with difficulty, his Latin
pride giving a stiffness to the words. 'I drank too
much, I was not—myself.'

Laura restored lipstick and comb to her bag
before turning coolly to face him, her eyes a
frosty blue. 'That's just the point, Román;
perhaps that *was* the real you. I don't know you
well enough to judge, and that speaks for itself,
doesn't it? We don't know each other well enough
to pledge our lives to each other, and that's what
marriage means to me, a lifetime commitment.'
Her voice thickened as she strove for control.
'May I borrow the car to drive back to Chapala
and pick up my parents and my things?'

For a moment he made no reply, his mouth
seeming too tight to let words escape, then he

forced them out like granite pebbles. 'Have you forgotten that there may be consequences of what happened last night? A child. . .'

She forced a laugh, though that contingency hadn't occurred to her as yet. 'Haven't you heard? Unwanted children can be disposed of as easily as any other undesirable trash.' She wanted to hurt him as deeply as he had wounded her, and knew she had succeeded when his face blanched to an even deeper whiteness, making the dark wings of his eyebrows, the black shock of his hair stand out in contrast.

Nevertheless, control etched his words as he said tautly, 'I will drive you to Chapala.'

'I can drive myself——'

'I will drive you to Chapala.'

It was natural to hate the man who had forced himself upon you and taken by savagery the tender essence of your being, wasn't it? Laura's intellect told her this was so, but the miserable lump of sadness lodged in her breast refused to budge to intellectual reason as the car swept past hills lit by the iridescent glow that pierced the clouds of mist covering the gently contoured hills on the road to Chapala.

For the first time she wondered about her parents' reaction to her sudden decision to call off the wedding. Their loyalties would lie with her, their only daughter, but long years in the Diplomatic Service would temper their allegiance with an unwillingness to offend a foreigner who had sought to become their son-in-law. Particularly a foreigner with Román's obvious assets and influence. How eminently suited her

parents were to their role in life was made evident
as soon as she set foot in the faintly dusty hall of
the Villa Vista.

'Darling,' her mother came forward from the
living room overlooking the sun-streaked lake,
'we wondered what had happened to you. You
really shouldn't go off like that and not let us
know your destination.' Her eyes crinkled in a
knowing smile over Laura's shoulder to the man
who had followed her in. 'I understand your
eagerness to be together, but it's only a few days
to the wedding, after all.'

'There isn't going to be a wedding,' Laura said
jerkily. 'We—Román and I—decided to wait a
while. Explain it to Daddy, will you?' she ended
pleadingly, seeing her father emerge from the
living room, an air of complacent satisfaction
about him, as if the hours he had spent assuring
his wife of their daughter's safety and happiness
had suddenly borne fruit.

Laura darted across the hall and scarcely felt
the stairs under her feet as she raced for the
sanctuary of her room. Later she could face the
questions, the bewilderment, the embarrassment,
but not now. Several minutes passed before she
remembered that the lattice panes she leaned
against looking out to the glistening lake
belonged to Román; she no longer had the right
to gaze possessively on the fulsome blossom of
rosebeds, the soft green of lawns leading down to
the debris-strewn lakeside. She had seen herself
as mistress of that smooth grass nurtured by
copious amounts of water, the *châtelaine* of
Román's domains here at Lake Chapala, the Villa
Castillo in Guadalajara, the home she had not yet

seen in Mexico City . . . now they were like half-forgotten dreams, pictures painted by an inexperienced hand.

She stirred lethargically when a soft tap sounded at her door, the view from the window she leaned against more tangible than the sound of her mother's softly modulated voice.

'Laura? I don't want to intrude on your privacy, but I just want you to know that I'm here if you need me.' She paused before going on tactfully, 'I've talked with Román, and he seems to understand how you feel. I must confess that it's all a mystery to me, though I can't pretend I'm not just a little relieved that you've decided to wait a while.' Her voice gentled with sympathy, she went on, 'You really don't know each other very well, do you?'

'No,' Laura choked, returning her gaze to the view, which was now blurred from the tears filling her eyes. 'We've—decided never to marry . . . it was all a mistake from the beginning. Román is—different from what I thought, he—he's. . .' Her voice trailed off in misery, and she was unaware of the sharp look her mother directed at her averted head.

'Darling,' Eleanor said eventually, reluctantly, 'I know we don't talk much about it, but sex is very important in the man-woman relationship. Not the most important, but it's high up there in the list of requirements for happiness.' Awkwardly, she added, 'If whatever happened between you and Román last night shocked you, I mean——'

'I really don't want to talk about it right now, Mother,' Laura stated flatly, the tears gone as she turned to face Eleanor again. 'It's over, and all I want to do is leave Mexico far behind me. Do you mind having your vacation cut short? We could spend Christmas somewhere else?—Nassau, somewhere like that,' she ended vaguely.

'How about home, in Washington?' Eleanor suggested softly. 'I'm sure your dad would like that better than anything.'

Wordlessly, Laura hugged her mother, the tears rising again making it impossible to speak. All she needed at that moment was the blessed security of people who loved her without question, as her parents did. The immediate future was taken care of; by the time they had to leave America on their last assignment, she would have put Román and Mexico far behind her, physically and emotionally. . .

Despite the zero temperatures outside Laura's New York apartment, it seemed incredibly stuffy as she rolled another sheet of virgin white paper into the typewriter. Maybe it was because she was writing about the high-altitude heat of Guadalajara, she thought lethargically, and that would explain the sleepiness too, as if she were living again those first days at the Villa Castillo.

The book was going well, and helped in her waking hours to expunge the memory of Román and what might have been, despite her mental involvement with his surroundings. She could motivate her hero much more realistically now, having known Román—or had she really known him? The part of him she had loved haunted her dreams, so that often she awoke with a smile that reflected the sensual satisfaction of her unconscious yearning, her arms embracing the pillow which had seemed in her dream to be Román's tightly knit body.

With an effort of will, she forced her attention back to Maria Delgado, the wife of aristocratic Felipe Alvarez, who was now expecting the child of her arrogant, womanising husband. The symptoms of pregnancy were a closed book to Laura, but she substituted the way she had been feeling herself lately . . . vaguely nauseous in the morning, blaming her sickness on whatever she had eaten for dinner the night before and resolving to better her diet; yesterday she had become so faint on the walk she disciplined herself to take each day that a man, a stranger, had noticed and helped her back to the entrance of her apartment building. Did all writers identify that much with their characters? she wondered.

She had identified Román with the hero of her novel at first, then reversed her opinion before changing it back again. What more natural than that she should identify herself with the morning sickness of Maria Delgado?

Leaning her arms on the typewriter, Laura stared through the window on her left and saw nothing of the undulating New York rooftops where snow had melted in patches according to where the building's heat was concentrated. Maria wasn't the only one pregnant . . . her own symptoms paralleled her fictional character's too closely not to be genuine. Her own brittle response to Román's voicing such a possibility returned to haunt her. She had said something about trash being easy to dispose of. But this wasn't trash ... a new human being even now joined its heartbeat with her own, drawing sustenance from her bone and fibre. Conscious recognition of her state simply reinforced her vaguely held belief that life was precious, even this one which had been conceived in anger and hate.

There was no stigma attached nowadays to a child born out of wedlock ... Laura admitted to herself that she wouldn't have cared about that in any case. A warm, nurturing feeling, which a psychologist friend of hers would have said was a manifestation of the Madonna complex, filled every crevice of her being. She would bear the child and bring him up unaided by his father.

Her mouth twisted in irony. Román's Latin philosophy had invaded her own thinking ... a male child took precedence over a female. But she didn't care about that, she told herself fiercely. A daughter would be equally, if not more, acceptable to her. Projecting into the future, she saw a solemn black-eyed teenager who would be moulded in her own image, not her father's...

Her child was an accepted part of her existence when, a month later, Laura looked up irritably from her typewriter to stare at the door which led directly into her living room from the lobby outside. Damn David, who lived on the floor below and ignored her pointed desire to be alone to finish her book. She was tidying up the last chapter of the tome she hoped would represent security for herself and her child for some time to come.

She padded across to the kitchen and filled a

cup with sugar before crossing to the door, smiling a little grimly as she mused thoughtfully that perhaps her neighbour would take the hint. 'Take the sugar excuse for a visit, and leave me alone to finish my work.' Uncaring of her appearance in faded jeans and blousy top, her hair tumbling haphazardly round her face, she grasped the handle of the door with one hand and thrust the cup of sugar forward with the other.

'Hello, and goodbye,' she said determinedly as the door swung open—and then her jaw dropped similarly open. It wasn't the promising art student, David, who stood on the threshold looking faintly bewildered. It was Román, precisely dressed in dark suit and immaculate white shirt, looking faintly foreign as he filled the doorway.

His eyes went from hers to the incongruously offered cup of sugar. 'I admit my nature might need sweetening from time to time,' he acknowledged mildly, 'but I would not have thought that fact was so obvious.'

Laura was too frozen to speak. The sugar-filled cup remained extended as her mind sought desperately to make sense of this sudden visitation. How had he known where to find her?—why had he found it necessary to do so?

'I——' Aware of the cup held out at arm's length, Laura lowered it in embarrassment. 'Please come in,' she invited jerkily, her heart beginning to beat erratically as she closed the door behind him and went quickly to deposit the offending cup out of sight on the counter of the kitchen that filled the lower third of the living room. She was conscious of the dust accumulated on the furniture, but more aware of her own dishevelled appearance as she led him into the seating area. She bent quickly to lift several heavy tomes from the armchair she indicated he should take. 'Can I offer you a drink?' she asked, sure that the heavy thrum of her heart must be audible to his perfectly formed ears. 'I haven't much— just a little white wine, or instant coffee,' she ended desperately, berating herself for not supplying a more sophisticated drink list before reason took over. How often did she entertain a man of Román's worldly tastes? Never.

'Not coffee,' he grimaced, indicating his dislike of the American brew over Mexican. 'Perhaps a little wine?'

As she tremblingly filled two bowl-shaped glasses from the bottle extracted from a cupboard above the counter—there had been no time for niceties like chilling—Laura wondered frantically what had brought him here. Not even her mother knew of her condition, so he hadn't come in response to a desperate plea to make an honest woman of Eleanor's daughter. Maybe his far-flung business enterprises had brought him to New York, and he had decided to squander an hour or so on the woman who had almost become his wife. It was far too early yet to feel movement, according to the medical books she had been devouring lately, yet she felt her womb leap in a biblical sense. It was too ridiculous to believe that her child leapt in recognition of its father, but she nevertheless offered a prayer of thanks that her smock-like top concealed the undone button fastening her jeans to her waist as she walked unsteadily back into the room where he sat. Román would always look at home wherever his handsomely contoured bones found themselves . . . he looked supremely at ease as she placed his glass on the small table to his right, his black eyes courteously interested as they lit on her typewriter and the scattered pages surrounding it.

'You are working on your novel set in Mexico?' he asked politely.

'Yes—it's coming along very well.' As a defence against the stilted words, Laura attempted a hardboiled nonchalance as she seated herself on the rocker set at right angles to his chair.

'I never did show you the historical maps and information I have, did I?' he asked so softly that she was taken unawares.

'No, I—I guess you didn't. But I'm managing just fine without that kind of authentic detail,' she rallied in justification. 'Our libraries here have a surprising amount of historical data.'

Román nodded agreeably, his black eyes lighting on hers only briefly. 'I am glad you have found what is necessary,' he commented politely, increasing the stilted atmosphere between them so that Laura felt like screaming.

'How did you know where to find me?' she asked bluntly, too nauseated even at this time of day to fortify herself with wine. Her glass lay untouched on the round table beside her.

'I knew I was to visit New York on business,' he informed her smoothly, 'so I contacted your mother at the address Tia Isabel gave me, and,' he shrugged, 'here I am.'

'How is Tia—Señora Castillo?' Laura corrected politely.

'She is well. More so since I sent Nicolas to represent the company in Los Angeles. It seems that mothers worry less about their offspring when they are separated by a thousand miles or so.' His tone was lightly facetious, but Laura felt a deep pang within her. She would never feel happy at separation from the child growing within her ... they would always mean all-in-all to each other. That was yet another reason to keep her pregnant state hidden from Román ... it hardly seemed likely that he would want the child conceived in such a way, but if the fancy took him, his status and influence would find the means to deprive her of her child, which had already become the focus of her existence.

'It's not as if Nicolas were a child,' she injected in defensive argument. 'Children need to be with their mother, but once they're grown——' she shrugged, unable to look ahead to the day when her child would leave her to make his or her way in the world.

'Tia Isabel has spoiled him almost beyond redemption,' Román dismissed shortly, his black eyes roving around the room and coming to rest on the pile of books she had removed from his chair. 'You are interested in medical matters?' he inquired politely, swivelling his gaze back to her again and drawing hot colour into her cheeks as she berated herself for leaving titles like *The Expectant Mother* and *The Single Parent* lying around for anyone to see.

'I need information for my book,' she ad-libbed hastily. 'Can I get you more wine?'

'Thank you, no. Like you, I have scarcely touched the first glass.' His eyes touched lightly on the pale liquid in her glass before coming up to meet her eyes, then sweeping rapidly down over her smocked figure, shock flashing momentarily in their black depths. When he once more raised his gaze to hers, his eyes were narrowed, obscuring whatever expression they held. Laura's heart fluttered in panic; she was sure he suspected something.

She sprang to her feet and said with false regret, 'Well, it's been nice to see you again, Román, but I really do have to get back to my writing—perhaps next time you're in New York we'll have a longer visit together.'

She was talking confusedly, too urgently demanding that he leave. Román stood up and came towards her without haste, an inexplicable expression in his darkly glowing eyes. Her breath caught in a gasp as his hand came out and touched the fullness of her breast before reaching down under her smock to feel the rounded hardness of her abdomen, the telltale gape of the unfastened top button of her jeans. Through her confusion, a sensual thrill rippled through her at the touch of his long, lean fingers on her body.

'You are having a child—my child,' he stated flatly, though a new element had entered his voice. Laura distractedly interpreted it as being matter-of-fact businesslike, the voice of a man who would not hesitate to deprive her of the main reason for her existence. New emotions sprang into being inside her . . . this child was hers, not his in any but a biological sense. He had come here to check his earlier diagnosis and found himself right in his conjecture. Why else would he have waited four months to make his seemingly casual visit?

'Why should you think the child is yours?' she attempted a smart nonchalance, realising that it was useless to deny her condition. 'I'm not one of your tradition-bound Mexican women——'

'Nor are you a believer in promiscuity,' Román cut in decisively, bewildering her with the intensity of the glow that seemed to have been ignited somewhere deep inside him to flame visibly in his eyes. It was as if—as if becoming a father satisfied some deep and long-hidden urge within him. Hope surged through her and sent her pulses pounding, then dwindled to a flicker. He was pleased because it was his child she carried, not because he loved her, its mother.

'The child is mine,' she said in a flat voice that cracked drily in her effort to control her resentment of his power and confidence, even the irrepressible smile that played at the corners of his well-shaped mouth.

'And mine,' he reminded her softly, his arms reaching round her to bring her to the pulsing warmth of his body. 'We will be married at once,' he decided against her ear with characteristic disregard for her feelings. 'Then perhaps a honeymoon on a Caribbean island?'

It took an effort of will to detach herself from his warmly enfolding grasp, and she saw the puzzled frown that sliced between his black brows as she turned away. She felt suffocated by the surge of longing that ripped through her. If only things had turned out differently . . . if only the love that had begun to blossom between them had pursued its natural course . . . if only

Gavin's stupidity hadn't roused Román's distrust of her as his woman. . .

'I won't marry you because I'm expecting your child,' she said wearily. 'I—appreciate your offer, but please . . . leave us alone.' She unconsciously included the child in her plea for solitude.

'What are you saying?' Román queried harshly, bringing her eyes round to stare at him numbly. 'You think I came here because of a child I did not know existed? I came because I could no longer stand the emptiness in my life, the absence of your beautiful presence at the Villa Castillo, the sound of your voice that echoed through the hall and almost sent me mad with longing for you. I care about the child you carry because it is part of you and part of me, not for itself alone. I came not knowing how you would receive me after I treated you so abominably . . . that I was mad with jealousy was no excuse. Can you believe that I hurt myself much more than I injured you that night?'

Looking up into his face, so close now he had mended the gap between them, Laura did believe him. The schooled politeness he had displayed until now no longer existed; instead, he was a man with all his emotions showing in all their rawness, from the tight clench of his jaw to the open blaze in his eyes. She knew he would never expose himself this fully ever again to her eyes, and her arms opened to welcome him as he took a hesitant step towards her.

'I love you, Laura Benson,' he murmured close to her ear when a few moments had passed in a blissful, silent communion of one soul reaching for another. 'Will you marry me and be my wife, my heart, my reason for existing?'

And Laura, quickly re-adjusting her basic values which had recently made her child her own driving motive, said, 'Yes, Román, I'll marry you. Not because of the child, but because I—I love you too.'

The flame tree's blossoms had grown less fulsome, less fiery in the intervening months since Laura had stood under them, but the tree gave off a lethargic mood of resting, of gathering force for the new life gestating within it. As the new buds burst forth, Laura too would give birth to new life.

A sigh of contentment breathed through her lips. The cycles of life were somehow more pronounced here in Mexico's central plateau, where extremes of weather were unknown, every season gently taking its course. Her New York apartment, sub-leased to a new tenant, seemed remote in time, so much had happened since that significant day of Román's visit.

The child burgeoning within her had in-explicably taken second place in her priorities on their honeymoon in a secluded villa in Jamaica, where a turquoise sea had beckoned them from the azure blue of the pool attached to the villa. Laura had forgotten the thickening of her waistline as Román made love with the deep passion of his warm blood on the pure white sand, the sinking comfort of their king-sized bed in the villa . . . each day, each night, brought her a little more knowledge of the man who was her husband. Then, he had devoted every waking hour to her, and even some of the night hours, when he would reach in his sleep to draw her to the hard curve of his gold-tanned body as if to reassure himself of her presence.

A small frown creased her smooth forehead. It had been different since their return to the Villa Castillo, for Román had been immediately immersed in business. A business life that she resented because it excluded her. It was foolish to feel that way, she knew, since Román had no objection to her literary ambitions ... her book about Felipe Alvarez and the ill-fated Maria Delgado had been well received by the critics, who were fulsome in their praise of the new literary light on the world scene. Perhaps once the baby was born she would start to plan another book. For now she felt delightfully free of encumbrances like that.

Warm lean fingers ran over the bareness of her arms, and she turned instinctively to face Román, a smile beginning from the corners of her mouth and radiating outward to encompass the honey-gold of her facial skin.

'Darling,' she murmured, letting her fingers linger with sensual touch over the hard muscled contours of his shoulders, 'I thought you'd never get here.'

He kissed the cool pink curve of her ear, his breath warming it like a benediction. 'I might as well spend every hour of every day with you, my love, because even in a business meeting my thoughts stray towards you, wondering what occupies you, what thoughts you are thinking in that beautiful head.'

'This beautiful head,' she retorted with irony, 'is wondering if you'll be home in time to greet our guests. There are some very important people coming for dinner tonight,' she reprimanded severely, though her hand went instinctively to smooth the hair back from his tanned forehead.

'They could not be half as important as you, *cara*,' he said huskily at her ear, his breath stirring the slow fire that his touch always evoked. 'Why don't we cancel the dinner and spend the evening together? I can think of many things to amuse you.'

With a gurgle of laughter, Laura pushed him to arm's length. 'I'm sure you can,' she said huskily, 'but our guests are due in fifteen minutes from now—too late to cancel.'

His curse was only half-hearted as he stepped away from her; she knew as he stepped confidently towards the patio that she possessed only half of him. The rest was given to the cut and thrust of the business world that had formed the man he was. He would always be hers in the deepest sense, but other interests would make him inaccessible from time to time.

She would take her lesson from the flame tree, which bided its time before bursting forth into the beauty it was intended to convey. . . .

A tempting offer from Mills & Boon

Temptation is a new kind of romance from Mills & Boon. Exciting, sensuous, compelling... written for today's woman. Two new titles will be published every month, starting in February.

SPECIAL INTRODUCTORY PRICE
ONLY 99p EACH

And to make Temptation totally irresistible, the February and March titles can be yours for the special introductory price of just 99p.

Go on – give in to Temptation.

The Rose of Romance

ROMANCE

Variety is the spice of romance

Each month, Mills & Boon publish new romances. New stories about people falling in love. A world of variety in romance — from the best writers in the romantic world. Choose from these titles in March.

WRECKER'S BRIDE Kathryn Cranmer
RING OF CRYSTAL Jane Donnelly
OUT OF WEDLOCK Sandra Field
NEVER KISS A STRANGER Mary Gabriel
THE HABIT OF LOVING Rosemary Hammond
THE FLAME TREE Elizabeth Graham
THE PASSIONATE LOVER Carole Mortimer
DRAGON MAN Elizabeth Oldfield
NO TIME FOR MARRIAGE Roberta Leigh
THE ROAD Emma Goldrick

On sale where you buy paperbacks. If you require further information or have any difficulty obtaining them, write to: Mills & Boon Reader Service, PO Box 236, Thornton Road, Croydon, Surrey CR9 3RU, England.

Mills & Boon
the rose of romance

 **ROMANCE**

Next month's romances from Mills & Boon

Each month, you can choose from a world of variety in romance with Mills & Boon. These are the new titles to look out for next month.

TEMPORARY HUSBAND Susan Alexander
LADY WITH A PAST Lillian Cheatham
PASSION'S VINE Elizabeth Graham
THE SIX-MONTH MARRIAGE Penny Jordan
ICE PRINCESS Madeleine Ker
ACT OF POSSESSION Anne Mather
A NO RISK AFFAIR Carole Mortimer
CAPTIVE OF FATE Margaret Pargeter
ALIEN VENGEANCE Sara Craven
THE WINGS OF LOVE Sally Wentworth

Buy them from your usual paperback stockist, or write to: Mills & Boon Reader Service, P.O. Box 236, Thornton Rd, Croydon, Surrey CR9 3RU, England. Readers in South Africa write to: Mills & Boon Reader Service of Southern Africa, Private Bag X3010, Randburg, 2125.

Mills & Boon
the rose of romance

Masquerade Historical Romances

From the golden days of romance

Picture the days of real romance – from the colourful courts of mediaeval Spain to the studied manners of Regency England. Masquerade Historical romances published by Mills & Boon vividly recreate the past. Look out for these superb new stories this month.

RACHEL AND THE VISCOUNT
Alanna Wilson

THE POLISH WOLF
Janet Edmonds

Buy them from your usual paperback stockist, or write to: Mills & Boon Reader Service, P.O. Box 236, Thornton Rd, Croydon, Surrey CR9 3RU, England. Readers in South Africa-write to: Mills & Boon Reader Service of Southern Africa, Private Bag X3010, Randburg, 2125.

Mills & Boon
the rose of romance

Take 4
Exciting Books
Absolutely
FREE

Love, romance, intrigue... all are captured for you by Mills & Boon's top-selling authors. By becoming a regular reader of Mills & Boon's Romances you can enjoy 6 superb new titles every month plus a whole range of special benefits: your very own personal membership card, a free monthly newsletter packed with recipes, competitions, exclusive book offers and a monthly guide to the stars, plus extra bargain offers and big cash savings.

AND an Introductory FREE GIFT for YOU.
Turn over the page for details.

As a special introduction we will send you four exciting Mills & Boon Romances Free and without obligation when you complete and return this coupon.

At the same time we will reserve a subscription to Mills & Boon Reader Service for you. Every month, you will receive 6 of the very latest novels by leading Romantic Fiction authors, delivered direct to your door. You don't pay extra for delivery — postage and packing is always completely Free. There is no obligation or commitment — you can cancel your subscription at any time.

You have nothing to lose and a whole world of romance to gain.

Just fill in and post the coupon today to **MILLS & BOON READER SERVICE, FREEPOST, P.O. BOX 236, CROYDON, SURREY CR9 9EL.**

Please Note:- **READERS IN SOUTH AFRICA write to Mills & Boon, Postbag X3010, Randburg 2125, S. Africa.**

FREE BOOKS CERTIFICATE

To: **Mills & Boon Reader Service, FREEPOST, P.O. Box 236, Croydon, Surrey CR9 9EL.**

Please send me, free and without obligation, four Mills & Boon Romances, and reserve a Reader Service Subscription for me. If I decide to subscribe I shall, from the beginning of the month following my free parcel of books, receive six new books each month for £6.60, post and packing free. If I decide not to subscribe, I shall write to you within 10 days. The free books are mine to keep in any case. I understand that I may cancel my subscription at any time simply by writing to you. I am over 18 years of age.

Please write in BLOCK CAPITALS.

Signature _____

Name _____

Address _____

_____ Post code _____

SEND NO MONEY — TAKE NO RISKS.
Please don't forget to include your Postcode.

Remember, postcodes speed delivery. Offer applies in UK only and is not valid to present subscribers. Mills & Boon reserve the right to exercise discretion in granting membership. If price changes are necessary you will be notified.

6R *Offer expires June 30th 1985*

EP86